HIS HEART'S
SECOND SIGH

ROSIE CHAPEL

ULFIRE PTY LTD

First printing: 2019
ISBN: 978-0-6485283-8-8

Ulfire Pty. Ltd.
P.O. Box 1481
South Perth
WA 6951
Australia

www.rosiechapel.com

Cover artwork by Lisa Miller with Got You Covered

❀ Created with Vellum

For those who refuse to allow age to define them... this is for you

ACKNOWLEDGMENTS

My endless gratitude to Melanie, Amy, Jackie, Julie, Maria, Brian and Lilly. Thank you for putting up with my nonsense and allowing me to bounce ideas off you – you have no idea how much your friendship means to me.

Heartfelt appreciation to Lisa for this gorgeous cover – your ability to create exactly what I am imagining, never ceases to astonish me!

To Graham from *A Fading Street Publishing*, thank you for your expert editing.

To my awesome husband... thank you for your love, patience – long-suffering though it may be – and unfailing support.

1

Reuben Faulkner stared at the papers spread out on the desk in front of him. All those years, and nothing, then... out of the blue... this. He couldn't decide how he felt but guessed he shouldn't be surprised. Leaning back in the chair he pinched the bridge of his nose, trying to release some of the tension. He would have to tell Jake. News of this magnitude could not be ignored or pushed under the table. Plus, he had a right to know — she was his mother after all.

Standing, Reuben walked over to gaze out of the window onto the stark beauty of the wintry garden with unseeing eyes. His vision was turned inward to the day before Erin left.

Thirty-four years earlier.

"Please Ben, just for once can we do something *I* want to do?" Erin's tone had taken on a grating, whiny quality, causing Reuben to frown.

"You know I can't get leave in the middle of semester, sweetheart. It's only a couple of months and we'll have the whole of the summer. We can go then. I can probably wangle six weeks."

"Yeah, you say that now, then there'll be a conference, or a dig or something you just *have* to attend or lead. Face it, Ben, you're more interested in lecturing and your PhD research than me."

Reuben gaped at the unfairness of his wife's accusation. "Erin, that's not true. We take holidays every year, none of which have remotely involved archaeology or conferences." His thoughts winging to their last break, less than three months ago, when they'd visited her family and toured California. "We just came back from a month in the States. I can't afford to go away every few weeks, love. You knew that when you married me. I am not some rich oil tycoon."

Erin pouted and, closing the gap to her husband, stretched up to brush a kiss to his lips, simultaneously walking her fingers up his shirt, fiddling with the buttons. Reuben drew her against him to kiss her long and thoroughly, the ever-present desire flaring. At the same moment Erin began to undo his shirt, they were disturbed by a wail.

"Every time, it's like he knows... brat," Erin complained.

Reuben chuckled and disentangled himself. "Wait here, he probably just needs settling." He strolled along to the nursery, to spy their son standing at the rails of the cot, scrubbing his nose with his fist, his face flushed with temper. "What's up, Jake?" Reuben lifted the child into his arms, taking the opportunity to rest the back of his hand on Jake's forehead. It felt a little warm but not overly so. "Did you have a bad dream?" he cooed, rhetorically, while rocking the child gently.

Jake snuggled into his father, nudging his head under

Reuben's chin. In minutes he was fast asleep again. Reuben laid him carefully in the cot, and tucked a sheet around him, before covering half of his stocky little body with the blanket so he would not get hot. He stood for moment studying his son. The familiar yet inexplicable joy, he was somehow partly responsible for producing such a perfect child, washed over him and, unable to help himself, he ran a tender finger along Jake's cheek.

"He always responds better to you." Erin's voice drifted to him from the doorway. He turned to see his wife leaning on the door jamb, her lovely features marred by discontent. Reuben swallowed a sigh.

"Pure imagination, darling. He loves us both the same, it's just he sees me more because I drop him at the Uni childcare centre."

Erin, who hadn't worked a day since their marriage and had no other call on her time, refused to be a stay-at-home mother. She declared she had no intention of being tied to a kitchen sink or a squalling child. That's what day-care was for.

Thankfully, Reuben's job entitled him to make use of the childcare facility on campus and, although he hated leaving Jake there while he was lecturing, at least the child was well looked after. He felt the frown returning. Erin had changed so much. Gone was the carefree spirit he fell in love with. She was always irritated either with him or Jake, and he couldn't remember the last time she had done anything spontaneous, not even a smile. He didn't know what was wrong; when he asked, she shrugged and said she was fine.

He knew she chafed at the quiet of Moorview, their home in the village of Rosedale Abbey. She had begged him to move several times, but he could not bear to sell up. The Yorkshire moors were his solace and, especially after a busy term, his haven. They had talked about buying a flat in Durham, so Erin was closer to Newcastle and all it had to offer, but so far it had not come to fruition. Everything they looked at was too small.

Erin was from San Francisco. Her family's home was huge, two stories, with a tennis court and a pool. Compared with North Yorkshire, where the weather had a tendency to be unpredictable, San Francisco always seemed warm and sunny — quite attractive, he supposed, if you liked that sort of thing. Reuben much preferred the four definite seasons. In actual fact, when he really thought about it, Erin and he were vastly different in outlook. That was probably what drew them together, they were the epitome of opposites attract. They fell in love, at least Reuben had, but lately, he was not so sure about Erin. They married very young, and for the last four years he thought they were happy. He certainly was. As he scanned Erin's face, he realised she was miserable, and his heart cracked a little.

With a final glance at Jake to make sure he was asleep, Reuben walked over to his wife and took her in his arms. "I'm sorry, love. I know you struggle being here all day. How about we go check out some apartments this weekend?" He deliberately used the term Erin was more accustomed to, because it made them sound considerably larger than they actually were. "Might be worth going down to York and seeing what they have available. It'd be just as easy for me to get to work from there as here." He kissed her nose, her cheek, then scattered light kisses along her throat. He heard her sigh as she angled her head exposing the soft skin of her neck, and felt her fingers worming under his shirt.

Lifting Erin, Reuben carried her along to their bedroom and spent the next little while demonstrating just how much he loved her.

When he woke the next morning, she was gone.

At first, Reuben tried to persuade himself Erin had just decided to take an early morning stroll, or perhaps a drive. Hours ticked by and, with no evidence she was returning any time soon, he conceded his wife's disappearance was far more serious.

Even now, over three decades later, he recalled his sense of absolute shock and fury that she had walked away, after their night of passionate lovemaking. Then the questions began hammering into his mind. Why had she gone? Was there someone else? How had she managed to leave without him hearing her? What about Jake? Their beautiful son had slept through his father's panic, supremely oblivious to the confusion.

Reuben had rung his widowed mother, who dropped everything to come and stay. Sarah Faulkner never trusted Erin, whom she believed had anticipated being the wife of an academic would be glamorous. Lecture tours to exotic places, wining and dining in the hallowed halls of prestigious universities, black-tie balls, long holidays to faraway lands. Instead of which she found herself married to a hard-working, rather reserved lecturer, who enjoyed a peaceful existence on the edge of the moors and who, other than participating in the occasional archaeological dig, seldom left England. Children had not been part of Erin's plan either. She wanted to be free to come and go as she pleased, not be restricted by a pesky, needy, clingy rugrat... her words.

From the moment Jake was born, Reuben had done everything for their son. Even in the hospital, Erin showed little interest in the child she had brought into the world. She rarely held Jake, and Reuben could not recall her ever cuddling him, or rocking him to sleep when he was teething or unwell.

Now, just when Jake was about to turn three, his mother had upped and vanished.

When he looked back, Reuben could not fathom how he muddled through those first few days, which fast became weeks. He informed the police of Erin's disappearance and, after waiting the obligatory forty-eight hours — Erin was an adult and entitled to do as she pleased — they instigated a search. Her car was found at York train station and it was quickly established she had travelled to Kings Cross and onto Heathrow, where she had boarded a flight to San Francisco via New York. There the trail ended.

Reuben rang her family, sent letters, and telegrams. It was as though she had never existed, no one would tell him anything. Eventually, her grandmother bowed under his constant calls, and confirmed Erin was safe and well, but she wanted nothing to do with him. There was no accusation of ill-treatment, no claim he had not been a doting husband, Erin simply did not want to be married to him anymore.

Initially, Reuben had sent updates about Jake, but they petered out when he received no response. Neither did he hear from a lawyer with regards to Erin wanting a divorce. After a few years, she faded into the background. He did not forget her, he had loved her too much, but it was easier to cope if he consigned her to his past.

———

Now she was suddenly very much a part of his present.

2
_____

A door slamming and the sound of dogs barking jolted
Reuben back to his office at Moorview. Jake and Alex
were home, their return bringing an odd sense of relief, of
normality. He could deal with this.

Walking through to the kitchen, Reuben noticed the
table was groaning under the weight of several bags filled
with goodness knows what. Christmas was still a few weeks
away, but Alex liked to start preparing early. For someone
who until two years ago avoided any form of celebration,
Alex Faulkner had become almost obsessed with ensuring
this particular festival was perfect. It wasn't that they hosted
wild parties, or had large gatherings, in fact, for the most
part, it was just the three of them, but this year, Kassie and
Gabriel St Germain were coming. Alex was determined
nothing would be left to chance, or the last minute —
preparations for an imminent zombie apocalypse would
seem inadequate in comparison!

Alex, currently petting the five dogs who were winding
themselves around her legs yipping in delight, looked up at
Reuben's entry and greeted her father-in-law with a bright
smile.

"Sorry, Reuben. I think I got carried away, but the shops are full of so many wonderful things," she acknowledged ruefully, indicating the pile of bags. "The only thing left to get is the tree."

It was a long-standing tradition for the Faulkner household to go to one of the Christmas Tree farms. They would wander along the rows of pine trees inspecting each one, weighing up size over spread, and whether the branches would display the baubles to their best effect. There was always a stall serving hot mulled wine and other tasty treats to ward of the chill of a winter's afternoon — all in all a wonderful way to set the tone for the Christmas season.

"We should leave that until next week at the earliest, otherwise all the needles will have fallen off before we get to Christmas." Reuben tried to smile but it was not his best effort. "When you're sorted, may I have a word?" his request seemed casual, but even to himself he sounded flat. "I'll be in the office."

Alex and Jake exchanged puzzled glances when Reuben left the room.

"Go on, Jake. I'll make us all a coffee." Alex nodded towards the closed door. "Your dad might appreciate a private word. You can tell me later."

Jake smiled and dropped a kiss on her nose. "Sure?"

"Absolutely. I have never seen Reuben look so..." she paused, searching for the right word, "...defeated. Something is very wrong."

Drawing his wife close for a quick hug, Jake kissed her again, this time on the mouth, the moment lengthening.

Alex broke their kiss and leaned back, her eyes a little glazed. "Go on," she husked, shoving him in the chest, "this is not helping Reuben."

Jake grinned wickedly and patted her on the butt, then strolled out of the kitchen and along to the office. "What's happened, Dad?" he asked, as he walked into the room and shut the door behind him.

Reuben, standing by his desk, opened his mouth to speak, closed it again, and dropped into his chair. "This came today." He lifted a sheaf of papers and wafted them at his son.

Jake grabbed them and flicked through the sheets, too many to read quickly. A letterhead caught his eye and for moment his mind flew back two years, to when Alex had received the news about her parents, who had been killed in a freak accident. He had not been there for her, in fact, he almost lost her following a misunderstanding of which he had no awareness at the time. A cold finger traced down his spine and he made a concerted effort to read the words.

It was from a solicitor — no, an attorney — in California. In unemotional terms it declared Erin Faulkner was seeking a divorce on the grounds she and Reuben had been separated for more than five years. Attached herewith documentation proving the aforementioned separation... on and on it went. Jake couldn't take it in. Never mind coffee, he would need to sit down with a large whisky and peruse it properly.

"What the hell, Dad?" Jake's voice reflected his shock. "I assumed you asked her for a divorce years ago."

"Never got around to it, I suppose I thought..."

"What that she'd come to her senses and decide she couldn't live without us?" Jake's bitter tones echoed around the room. He paused, dampening down his anger. "Dad, *she* was the one who walked away. After seven years, you could have had her declared dead." He began pacing the room, unable to vent his frustration.

"I know, son, I know." Reuben raised his palms placatingly. "And no, I couldn't, I knew where she was and that she was alive. In all honesty I just forgot."

"Forgot? How could you for—?" Jake stopped his pacing and studied Reuben. His father looked as though he'd been punched. "What are you going to do?" An unpleasant thought struck him. "What is she after? Has she heard about your new book? I guarantee she's seen some of the publicity online or a TV report, and thinks she's entitled to some of your royalties?" Jake knew he'd hit a nerve when he saw the muscle in Reuben's jaw tighten. "Well she can sing for that. We have proof she abandoned us."

"Jake surely she can't exp—?"

"Of course, she can," Jake interrupted. "You're still married. Geez, Dad!"

At that moment the door swung open, to reveal Alex bearing coffees. Catching Jake's last words, she paused in the doorway. This was none of her business, but she loved both men, currently glaring at each other. Reuben had become the father she always dreamed of, and Jake... well he was her heart. Unsure, she hesitated, thinking it was best to leave them to it.

Reuben spotted her. "It's fine, Alex, come on in, you'll need to know what's going on, and Jake will tell you anyway. Erin has served me with divorce papers."

Alex was so surprised, her mouth fell open. "Wait... you're not already divorced?" Reuben shook his head. "Okay, well, just make sure you read it thoroughly, sign and return, unless you... surely you aren't... oh, Reuben. May I read the papers?" she asked, putting the tray down.

Reuben nodded, and Jake handed the documents to his wife.

Perching against the edge of the desk, Alex began to read, while Reuben and Jake sipped their drinks. Although not wholly conversant with legal jargon, she had a grasp of the basics. It all seemed fairly standard and innocuous until she came to the section about division of assets. She raised her head and locked eyes with her father-in-law.

"She wants half." Alex heard Jake hiss when she said this, and saw Reuben's shoulders slump.

"Bloody, bugger and sod." Reuben groused.

"It's easy enough to contest. You can gather plenty of witnesses to attest to her abandonment when Jake was a child," Alex assured him. "In fact, give me ten minutes. Okay to use your office, Jake?" She asked her husband.

Jake nodded and the two men watched Alex stalk out of the room in a purposeful manner. Time ticked by. Jake went to make another coffee for the three of them, although he felt his father would do better with something stronger.

It was well over half an hour before Alex came back into the study, where she gulped down her lukewarm coffee, grinning her thanks at Jake who offered to make her fresh one.

"Love one, thanks. Right..." She turned to Reuben. "I know Richard..." referring to Richard Tomlinson, senior partner at the law firm of Tomlinson, Draper and Vaughan, and a personal friend, "...is property, but they have a department which handles divorce cases. I've scanned and emailed the documents. They'll read, discuss, and then contact us tomorrow. He thinks someone will come up to have a proper chat with you, probably on Monday.

"Alex. You don't need to do this. I'm sure I can handle it."

"I'm sure you can too, but Richard said the firm she's engaged are notorious for railroading the opposing side. You need a team acting on your behalf who are not emotionally involved and have no qualms about being aggressive in response. You are too caring, Reuben, and she does not merit a single penny from you, never mind half. *Half,* cheeky cow." Alex glowered at the papers in her hand, appalled Erin assumed she had any claim at all, her heart aching for Reuben and Jake.

Her husband came back into the room with three more steaming hot coffees — they would be floating in it shortly — and a plate of biscuits. "You okay, hon?" she asked, when Jake put down the tray and handed her one of the mugs.

"I will be when this is over. She has caused enough grief in this family. No more. What did Richard say? It was Richard you rang, wasn't it?" Jake replied, taking an educated guess.

Alex nodded and repeated what she told Reuben, after which, they drank the heady brew in silence each lost in contemplation.

"Well, there's nothing more we can do until this representative or whoever comes up on Monday. So, let's put it out of our minds and concentrate on what we have left to do before Kassie and Gabe arrive," Reuben said, in tones which brooked no argument.

Brow creased, Jake opened his mouth, but before he could say anything, he tasted the chocolate coating of a caramel wafer. Startled, he glanced at his wife, remembering at the same time to bite down, to keep the biscuit in his mouth.

"Later," Alex cautioned in undertones. "Don't you have those emails you wanted to deal with before lunchtime?" Her expression willed him to tread carefully, and Jake inclined his head ever-so slightly in acknowledgement. He and Reuben hardly ever came to blows, but this was unexpected, and they needed time to weigh everything up.

3

The next few days passed without further discussion of the letter or Erin. Reuben made it clear the topic was off limits until they had spoken to whoever arrived on Monday.

Late on Friday afternoon, Richard Tomlinson called to confirm a lawyer and a paralegal should be at Moorview by 1p.m. on Monday — trains, traffic, and weather permitting. Reuben spent the weekend gathering any paperwork he thought might be required, while Alex and Jake carried on as though the bombshell had never been dropped.

Monday morning dawned bright but cold. The winter had been relatively mild to date, but the forecast was for the weather to deteriorate towards the end of the week, with heavy snowfalls predicted.

Reuben was so engrossed in research for his new book he scarcely registered the rap of the doorknocker just before one o'clock on Monday afternoon. Voices floated along the hall and, seconds later, Alex stuck her head around the door.

"Reuben, this is Lydia Struthers and her paralegal, Paige Latimer." Alex stepped to one side as two women followed her into the room. Reuben stood hastily and went to greet them.

"Pleased to meet you, Mr Faulkner. I'm Lydia and this is Paige." The first woman, a tall brunette wearing an expensive-looking power suit, came forward to shake Reuben's proffered hand.

"Thank you for taking the time to travel up from London, Mrs Struthers..." Reuben caught sight of Lydia's wedding ring and made the leap. "...and please, call me Reuben."

"Only if you return the favour and call me Lydia," she replied as she introduced Paige.

Reuben welcomed Paige with a smile and a handshake. "Lovely to meet you, too," he said and found himself staring at Lydia's paralegal. Paige Latimer was almost tall as he, which was a surprise — he was about 6'4". He could not guess her age but, given her position with the law firm, guessed she was probably in her late thirties. Golden-brown hair, neatly twisted into a bun, framed delicate features. Her eyes were an arresting shade — somewhere between blue and green — turquoise was the closest description Reuben could come up with and, throughout the afternoon, found his gaze kept straying to them. When her slender hand slid into his, Reuben was aware of an odd tingle snaking up his arm, gone so quickly, he presumed it was his imagination.

Alex, after asking whether the guests would like a coffee or tea, hurried away, to return shortly carrying a tray with two teas, one coffee and a plate of buttered, freshly baked, cheese scones. "I'll leave you to it, yell if you need me." She smiled and left, closing the door behind her.

. . .

There was a moment's silence when the door clicked shut.

Gathering himself, Reuben handed around the drinks and the three made themselves comfortable. Then Lydia spoke. She did not waste time with pleasantries.

"Right, I need every single piece of information you have pertaining to your marriage. Not just the legal documents, but the personal details, such as how long it lasted, when your wife left, why she left. Was there anything like abuse involved on either side, mental or physical? Did either of you have an affair? Has she been in contact at all since she left? Are there people who can attest to what did or didn't happen? When I say every detail, I mean absolutely everything, even those which might seem insignificant. I do not want any surprises. If, as Mr Tomlinson stated, Mrs Faulkner has been gone for thirty-odd years without any communication, this ought to be easy. However, divorce is an ugly game. People refuse to abide by the rules, neither do they like to be thwarted. If your wife is after some kind of monetary recompense, she will doubtless have a skeleton she can dig up or some mud she would like to sling."

Lydia pinned Reuben with a shrewd gaze.

"I need to tell you, warn you really, this will probably deteriorate into name calling and vengeful slurs. You have become quite a notable personality in your world, Professor," Lydia used his title, deliberately. She needed him to know this was not going to be a walk in the park. She had read the letter from Erin's attorney. On the face of it and given the circumstances, settlement ought to be reached promptly, but Lydia's years of experience had taught her never to assume anything associated with divorce would be quick or easy. She expected any negotiations would be protracted and difficult.

Reuben understood what Lydia was saying. "I just want this done, but I refuse to give in to Erin's demands. She left me, she abandoned me with a three-year old child, and severed all contact until last Friday. It took me months to discover she was alive after she disappeared, and that was only because her grandmother was sick of my constant phone calls. According to her, Erin simply did not want to be married to me anymore. She forfeited any right to anything of mine, including our son, the moment she walked out. I refuse to give her a brass razoo," Reuben stated emphatically, employing some Australian slang he'd picked up from a colleague.

His expression darkened, and he was hard pushed to keep his anger at bay. He took a steadying breath. "I had to bring up our son alone, and it was the hardest job I've ever done, as well as the most rewarding. I might be a professor now, but then I was just a lowly lecturer, paid a pittance. I couldn't afford nannies and babysitters. I was fortunate Jake was already in the crèche at uni and, when he went to school, I managed to schedule my lectures and tutorials around his timetable. Not once in the last nearly thirty-four years, has she made any attempt to see how he is. No, I'm done. She can throw anything she wants at me. I believe I have ample ammunition which I would be extremely pleased for you to throw right back."

While Reuben was venting his spleen, Paige Latimer observed him, quietly. On the journey up, while discussing the case, Lydia had asked her to study their new client. They needed to know his frame of mind, his sense of reason, his attitude towards this woman who was still his wife. Was he credible? Did it seem Erin had good reason to leave him in so hasty a manner? Was it an abusive situation? *Was* Erin, in fact, due some recompense, even after so many years. When Mr Tomlinson explained his connection to the Faulkners, he was very clear that, as far as he was concerned, the woman was simply money grubbing and needed squashing with all haste. The law was the law, however, and since Erin had engaged a company without scruples, they would need to be thoroughly prepped.

Reuben Faulkner was the polar opposite, from what Paige expected. When Mr Tomlinson mentioned he was professor, Paige had conjured up an image of a benign, forgetful, and rather staid man, whose students would fall asleep the minute he started speaking. Reuben was the antithesis of this.

She knew he was just the wrong side of sixty, but with his tanned face and shock of dark hair — with the merest smattering of grey threaded through it — he looked ten years younger. His eyes were greyish-blue, and he had the cutest laugh-lines which crinkled when he smiled. His voice was deep, with a tinge of his Yorkshire roots, but it was one she could listen to all day and never feel remotely bored.

In fact, she thought — as dispassionately as possible, a blush gliding up her cheeks — although not conventionally handsome, there was something compelling about Reuben's craggy, rather weather-beaten features. Arresting? Charismatic? Paige couldn't quite put her finger on it, but whatever it was piqued her interest... more than it should have done, given the situation.

Paige Latimer was happily single. She had only been in one long term relationship which ended six years previously, when she discovered her 'significant other' was cheating on her with at least three other women. Since then she hadn't avoided men as much as refrained from being part of or joining any kind of group, or club where she might meet one. One year shy of the big five-o, Paige was happy with her life and relished the fact, aside from her job, she was answerable only to herself. She could go on holiday when it suited her, she did not have to ask anyone's permission to decorate, or change furniture, or buy new clothes or eat out, or anything. She valued her independence and, until today, had never felt the urge to alter the status quo. When this tall, attractive stranger shook her hand, a curious sensation had trickled along her arm. Practically minded, Paige put it down to static, but in that moment, Reuben Faulkner, without even trying, had stirred something inside her — something long forgotten.

Unfortunately, not only was he their client, but also, he was about to go through what would likely be a nasty divorce. *Dammit all to hell!*

Paige pushed her wayward thoughts out of her head and concentrated on the matter at hand.

4

B y the end of the afternoon, Lydia was satisfied with what they had achieved. She now had a long list of people with whom she could speak regarding both Reuben's behaviour towards Erin, and vice versa. Character references and witness statements would also need to be arranged and, given it was over three decades ago, recall for some would, undoubtedly, be vague. Nevertheless, she intended to compile everything she could. Ammunition was the key. Erin would not get a penny, if Lydia could help it.

Watching the two women, while they prepared to leave, Reuben realised he wanted to extend their, well — if he was brutally honest — Paige's acquaintance. It was already dark, and he had no idea what their plans were for the evening, or whether they were returning to London on the late train.

"Would you like to stay for dinner?" The invitation was out before he had chance to think it through, but he had absolutely no intention of retracting it. "It saves you finding somewhere to eat in an unfamiliar place. There's the pub in the village which serves fantastic meals, but this is free and you're already here." He grinned engagingly.

Lydia and Paige exchanged a glance, and Lydia nodded. "Thank you, Reuben, that's very kind, we would love to. We're booked to stay in Thirsk overnight, because we weren't sure how long we'd be here this afternoon. Neither of us knows this area, so to have a home cooked meal is a bonus we didn't anticipate."

Paige added her thanks, and Reuben suggested they retire to the lounge, where they could enjoy a pre-dinner drink.

Jake and Alex were already there, surrounded by five dogs of varying ages and dubious heritage. The fire was crackling merrily, and Christmas music played quietly in the background.

Alex leapt off the sofa when they came in, and Reuben explained their London visitors were staying for dinner. "Hi again," she greeted them, "sit, sit, how lovely. It's Shepherd's Pie, hope that's okay." Not waiting for an answer, she headed for the kitchen to prepare more vegetables. Reuben followed her.

"Hope you don't mind the extra mouths, Alex. I didn't think, it just came out."

"Reuben, never apologise for inviting guests to dinner in your own home. You know we always have plenty to spare, and extra veggies take no time." She grinned and leant across to kiss his cheek. "How did it go?" Alex raised an eyebrow, while she tipped parsnips and sprouts into the sink and began to peel them.

Reuben gave Alex a brief rundown of the afternoon. "I

think we have enough to counter Erin's claim," he concluded.

"Of course, you do. How she can even think..." Alex shook her head, still dumbfounded at the gall of the woman. "Let's not dwell on it tonight, go make sure Jake is playing host. Oh, and there's some dip and crackers. You might put them on a tray... something to nibble on while dinner cooks."

Locating both crackers and dip, Reuben spread them haphazardly around a tray and returned to the lounge, where Jake, Lydia and Paige were discussing the pros and cons of London at Christmas.

The evening passed pleasantly. The visitors proved to be hilarious company and, for a while, the reason for their presence was forgotten.

Mid-evening, Reuben left them to it. One of the dogs wanted to go out, which meant they all did. While he waited for them do their business, he tidied the kitchen, stacked the dishwasher, washed the glasses, and put any dishes too big for the machine, in the sink to soak. He was elbow deep in soap suds when the kitchen door creaked open, and Paige stuck her head around.

"Want some help?" she offered.

"It's okay, I've got this, nearly done anyway. The rest can wait 'til morning. I just wanted to get them into water before the food dries like concrete." He smiled. Paige, spotting the tea-towel, joined him at the sink and dried the glasses Reuben had just rinsed.

"I'm quite useful with a tea-towel," she said, her mouth twitching at the sight of Reuben in a pinafore, arms covered in bubbles. "I don't imagine this is how most people picture a professor of ancient history and acclaimed author to boot." She swallowed the gurgle of laughter, threatening to spill over.

"Go on, laugh, my life is naught but drudgery and servitude," Reuben said with a sweeping bow, his tones deliberately overdramatic.

"Yeah, right," Paige chuckled as she placed a glass on the table. "I'll put these away if you want to point me to where they go."

"Not to worry, I can do that." Reuben leaned against the table, drying his hands, studying Paige. She intrigued him. She seemed self-possessed, yet her comments indicated someone with a wicked sense of humour. He moved around the table, opening a cupboard above the worktop and tucking the glasses onto the top shelf. The last one done, there was no reason to stay in the kitchen, but neither felt inclined to hurry back to the lounge. Paige twisted slightly in order to hang the damp tea-towel over the radiator, and as she turned back, came face to face with Reuben who was headed to check on the dogs. They did the dodge each other dance and, of course, both moved the same way, twice.

"You go," Paige grinned, standing to one side to let Reuben pass.

"Clearly, I need a bigger kitchen, not enough room to dance," Reuben chuckled.

"Oh, I think there's probably just enough..." Paige clamped her mouth shut and closed her eyes, feeling that frustrating heat inching up her cheeks. *Really? What are you playing at, Paige Latimer?*

Reuben halted in his tracks to stare at her, registering her heightened colour. They were so close he could see himself reflected in her eyes, which fluttered open again. He was definitely drawn to this newcomer with the glorious eyes, darker now under the electric light but no less bewitching. For the first time in longer than he could remember he actually wanted to kiss someone, to kiss Paige. Not just a brush of the lips, really kiss her until she was begging for more. He blinked, feeling his body slant towards her, wholly unable to prevent it.

A chorus of barks shattered the moment, and Reuben jerked back. He muttered something about bloody dogs and went to let them in, catching them at the door to wipe their feet before they put muddy paw prints on everything and everyone.

Paige remained motionless for seconds. He was going to kiss her. He was *actually* going to kiss her and, God help her, she desperately wanted him to. *How unprofessional could you get*? Worse, she wanted him to do more than kiss her. Her world seemed a little off balance and, rather than hang around — uncertain how to behave — Paige returned to the lounge. By the time Reuben rejoined them, dogs in tow, she was embroiled in a debate about the best Christmas movie.

Lydia and Paige left about an hour later, the former confirming she'd contact Reuben in the next few days.

"Everything will probably quieten down over the Christmas break," she said as the two were getting into their hire car. "I expect things will start to heat up in January. All I ask is, that you forward any letters or emails, in fact any communication at all you receive from Erin or her lawyers, to us, without responding. It is also better you don't read them. Ignoring the legalese, we all use to scare the opposition, these can be nasty missives, and people have a tendency to react without thinking. I'm sorry, that's just the way it is."

"No problem. I really don't want to get into a vindictive

dispute over this, I just want it over with. I should have done it years ago, but I had no clue where she was, or whether she was even still alive. To be frank, I think I hoped it would all just go away. Short-sighted of me, I know." Reuben opened his palms in an apologetic gesture. "I certainly never expected it to come to this."

"Not your worry now, Reuben, it's ours and we love a good fight." Lydia grinned. "Thank you for being so hospitable, I have enjoyed every minute. Paige." She nodded at her passenger who added her thanks. "I'll be in touch," she said as the window wound up and she turned the car in the driveway.

Reuben watched until the car drove out of sight, an odd feeling ghosting through him at the probability that was the first and last time he would encounter Paige Latimer.

Paige twisted in her seat, spotting the dark silhouette watching them leave. Her stomach plummeted, briefly, at the realisation she would likely never see Reuben Faulkner again.

5

C hristmas came and went. Kassie and Gabriel arrived with the first flurries of snow and were persuaded to stay until after New Year. The friends had a lot in common, ten days disappearing in a whirl of laughter, chatter and seasonal cheer. January blew in on a bitter wind, prompting Reuben to mutter he hoped it wasn't some ominous portent.

Festivities over, Jake returned to his fledging engineering consultancy, which had several contracts underway, and he predicted a busy year ahead. Alex and Reuben knuckled down to their own work. While researching Reuben's first book, the pair discovered one or two intriguing threads, inspiring a second volume. Reuben had been away much of the previous year, fulfilling his obligations to the publisher by delivering a series of guest lectures at universities around Europe and Australia. He had a dozen more lined up in the States along with numerous book signings and would be leaving in less than a month. One morning, at the end of the first week of January, Alex broached the subject.

"How are plans for the US lectures?" she asked, sipping the hot, strong coffee, Reuben had just brewed.

"All in hand, I presume. The publishing house and the American colleges are closed until next week, so I won't hear until they resume. As far as I know, I leave here on the twenty eighth of January and get back sometime towards the end of March." Reuben stood up from his desk and began to pace the floor. Unusually for someone who was normally pretty laid-back, he appeared troubled… agitated.

"What's up, Reuben?" Alex thought she knew what bothered him but didn't want him to think she was prying.

Reuben glanced at his daughter-in-law. "One of them is in San Francisco."

"Ahhh, home of the deeelightful Erin," she said with a trace of sarcasm and a questioning brow.

Reuben nodded. "I suppose at the back of my mind, I feel as though I should make the effort to contact her. Perhaps arrange to meet her, to discuss this mess. A way to keep it civil."

Alex bit down on her gut response, which involved very rude words. "Reuben, this is way past civil. If Erin wanted a nice quiet divorce, she would have sought one long ago. Yeah, she might have found someone else she wants to marry, but I reckon this is purely to take you for every penny she can squeeze out of you. I am convinced she has seen something about your minor celebrity status in the world of academia and thinks she can cash in on it. I'm pretty sure Lydia told you to have zero contact with her or her lawyers." Alex grinned, catching a guilty expression chasing across Reuben's face.

"She did, it's just…"

"I know, you loved Erin, maybe still do. You share a son, and don't want this to become acrimonious. Which is exactly why you should heed Lydia." When she said this,

Alex pondered the possibility of Erin turning up at a book signing and causing a scene. "Do you want me to come to America with you? I could run interference if Erin decides to show up."

Reuben chuckled at her fierce expression. "Thank you, Alex, no, I'll be fine. When I told Lydia, I had commitments in the States, she alluded to one of their staff being available to me. I presume from their New York office. And, no, I don't still love Erin. I admit, I did for a long time, even hoped she might come back, but all I feel now is indifference. I think the letter from her attorney's acted as a kind of catalyst. It brought me up sharp, forcing me take stock, and I realised I was in love with a memory, that's all. Whatever we shared is dead, it died a long time ago."

Alex got up from her chair, walked across to the window where Reuben was standing, and gave him a hug. "It'll be done with soon, and you can move on. Maybe even think about dating." She was astonished when Reuben flushed and bent his head, apparently finding the carpet fascinating. "Reuben?"

"Dating? Me? Give me a break." He put his empty coffee mug on the tray, sat down and to all intents and purposes looked to be immersed in ancient history. Alex might have been interested to know Reuben's thoughts were much closer to the present day, less than a month ago to be exact.

Paige Latimer was similarly occupied, her thoughts straying to Reuben Faulkner with unnerving frequency. He popped up with frustrating regularity and often at the most inconvenient moment. Paige was mildly irritated that the man, with whom she had spent mere hours, should take up so much of her mind. To complicate matters further, Lydia who had explained about Reuben's lecture tour and book signing, suggested Paige might like to accompany him as the representative from Tomlinson, Draper, and Vaughan.

Lydia could not absent herself for the period necessary, she had other clients. Paige's work, however, was more administrative and less 'shop front' so to speak, meaning she would be able to attend to any business while travelling. Paige was torn. On the plus side, it would give her more time with Reuben, conversely, it would give her more time with Reuben, acknowledging how ridiculous that sounded. She quite liked the man she had conjured up in her head, and the reality might shatter her illusion.

There was nothing she could do either way. If she was assigned to go with the professor, she wouldn't question it. Paige had never been to America, at the very least she might get in a bit of sightseeing.

―――――

By the end of the second week of January, all the plans were in place. When Lydia informed Reuben, Paige had been asked to act as a kind of liaison, he registered an unaccustomed lift of his spirits. If nothing else, because they would be thrown into each other's company, perhaps they could fit in some sightseeing. Reuben was tempted to suggest they travel together but decided against it. It seemed... precipitous to assume Paige would want to and, if he offered, she might feel obliged.

It was decades since he had dated, and Reuben wasn't even sure how it worked any more. According to various reports, documentaries, and TV shows, one would be forgiven for thinking people slept together at the drop of a hat these days. Reuben wasn't gullible enough to accept, at face value, everything he saw on the television, but accepted it was probably a trend. He preferred the idea of a slow courtship, a leisurely getting to know each other; to share kisses, maybe take it a bit further. One thing he hadn't believed in was sex before marriage.

Reuben shook his head. Talk about behind the times, he sounded like an idiot. What self-respecting woman would want to date him? *Date! God, it sounded so... juvenile*. He was no longer in his prime, he would be sixty-three on his next birthday... not a catch by any stretch of the imagination.

Bachelorhood had served him well for the last thirty-four years, he was happy for it to serve him for the next thirty-four.

6

_____

A month later, Reuben was halfway through his tour. His lectures at the various universities were delivered to packed auditoriums, and he was inundated with requests to sign copies of his book after each one. Conversely, the bookshop signings were relatively quiet. To be fair, despite international praise for his book, that acclaim was mostly within the academic sphere. A volume on the Emperor Hadrian, despite numerous high-quality images, was not considered 'light reading' — even on a rainy weekend. Nevertheless, he was excited to share his research and, so far, the feedback was positive.

Of Paige, Reuben had seen little. She stayed in the background, more a shadow in the wings than a companion. Thus far, they hadn't been able to arrange any sightseeing, because when he was free, she was busy catching up with her own work.

Three days ago, they had arrived in San Francisco, the one place Reuben could do with a friend, the one place it was probably better to seem unattached, even platonically. Paige was a beautiful woman and, although it was doubtful Erin would put in an appearance, Reuben didn't want to give his soon-to-be ex-wife any fodder, or place Paige in an awkward situation.

The previous two days had been spent at the history faculty of the University of San Francisco; the success of which had exceeded everyone's expectations. Four lectures across the two days, each with extra time available for questions and book signing, proved so popular, Reuben had been invited to return, to repeat the exercise towards the back end of the year.

Today he was doing a signing at The Bookshelf, which turned out to be a quirky bookshop, just off Market St. Within its sprawling interior there was also a café; books and coffee — two of Reuben's favourite things. He arrived half an hour early to be greeted by Joel, the aide assigned to him by the local branch of his publishing company.

Like clockwork, Joel turned up at every venue to help set up the table, unpack and stack the books, and make sure the signing portion of each event moved smoothly and quickly. Reuben, while appreciative of Joel's assistance was amused by this last requirement; especially at the bookshops. Half a dozen people wanting his signature wasn't exactly over-whelming, he could easily manage on his own. Still, he had to admit, he was glad of Joel's presence at the larger sessions.

"Coffee, Professor Faulkner," Joel said cheerfully, handing Reuben a large black coffee.

"Thank you, Joel, just what I needed. In fact, I'm not sure there'll be enough coffee to keep me going today. I need a day off." He feigned a grimace, making Joel laugh.

"One more day, sir and you have the whole weekend free."

"It cannot come soon enough. Don't get me wrong, these events are quite exhilarating, especially when people have a genuine interest in the content of the book, but I haven't been this busy in years. Never in my wildest dreams, did I anticipate a research volume on Hadrian would generate so much interest."

Joel shrugged. "It's easy to see why though, Professor, it's a fascinating book. The images alone would make it a best-seller, made all the more attractive because the language is not dry or stuffy. It makes the emperor come alive, if you don't mind my saying." He flushed a little when he spoke. Confessing to enjoying an academic tome was probably the least cool thing he'd done all month... all year.

Reuben grinned. "I'm glad you liked it, remind me to sign your copy before we part ways! Now, let's get this show started, shall we?" To Reuben's surprise, the area the manger had set aside filled rapidly, and soon it was standing room only.

Paige, who arrived at about the same moment Reuben began to speak, raised an astonished eyebrow at the crowd. Reuben dipped his head in her direction, then turning to face his audience, started his presentation. He spoke without notes, his brief synopsis of the book painting a vivid picture of Hadrian's life. Paige was riveted, it never got old, listening to Reuben. His passion for the historical period, not to mention his admiration of Hadrian himself was clear in his tone, and he never gave the same speech twice.

She leaned against the wall, studying the people hanging on his every word, many already nursing copies of his book. The mix of attendees was another eye-opener. Some, she surmised, were students but most looked like armchair historians. People who simply loved the subject and enjoyed reading everything they could get their hands on about any given topic relating to it.

A taller than average woman who had tagged onto the back of those standing, caught Paige's attention. Cautiously, she shifted position, allowing her to observe the newcomer without being obvious. Dark blonde hair, liberally scattered with salon-kissed highlights framed a tanned face, whose flawless features seemed... resentful was the best description Paige could think of.

Something niggled at the back of Paige's mind and, while the audience clapped their appreciation of Reuben's talk, it clicked. She remembered the photo Lydia had in the file and, despite the fact it had been taken almost forty years ago, Paige was pretty sure this was Erin Faulkner. How interesting. Deciding to keep a low profile — she didn't want Erin to jump to conclusions — Paige ordered a coffee and sat at the far side of the book shop, content to watch from behind a newspaper.

The woman assumed to be Erin hovered at the edge of the group milling around the table, queueing to get their books signed. Paige saw Joel approach her, holding a copy of Reuben's book. He said something and held out the book, but Erin — if indeed it was Erin — shook her head. Joel went back to running crowd control, while Erin spun on her heel, and headed towards the door. Halfway to the exit, she paused and swung back around, her eyes fixed on Reuben, who hadn't noticed her. He was laughing and chatting with his fans, his face wreathed in a cheerful smile. His shock of dark, shaggy hair kept falling across his face and his extraordinary eyes twinkled while he talked.

For someone who, until he started this book tour, only ever addressed university lecture halls, Reuben Faulkner was a natural at public speaking. He could hold an audience captive with his enthusiasm for his subject. With everyone he met, he never failed to sound genuinely interested in whatever they wanted to discuss, and made each person feel as though there was no one else he would rather be talking to in that moment. It was a rare gift, and Paige didn't think Reuben had the slightest clue he possessed it.

The woman waited until there were only a couple of people left in the queue, and moved forward.

Paige dithered between staying where she was, where any conversation would remain unheard, or joining her client so she could step in if necessary, to ensure nothing was said by either party which could be used against the other. Grumbling under her breath, Paige stood, and casually strolled around the shop until she was standing next to Joel.

"I think we might be in for some fireworks," she muttered for Joel's ears only.

Joel glanced at Paige in surprise "Why?"

"I do believe that is our esteemed author's not quite ex-wife." She nodded towards the woman.

"Oh my!" Joel's face was a picture. "Should I…"

Paige placed a restraining hand on his arm. "Let's just see what happens. I can handle her if needs be, but I daresay she has every right to speak to Reuben."

The two waited. The hub of the bookshop faded into the background as Reuben raised his head.

7

Reuben glanced up, glad to see the woman approaching the table was the last in the queue. He really wanted another coffee. His throat was dry, despite the copious amounts of water he had drunk during and after his talk, plus his hand was starting to ache from signing so many books. He was flabbergasted at the number of people who had attended, as well as how knowledgeable they were. Their questions insightful and broad ranging.

It had been a truly enjoyable experience and he made a mental note to thank the owner both personally, and in the press release they were preparing to run prior to his departure from America.

His eyes lifted to the woman's face and his jaw dropped. *Bloody bugger and sod! Here? Of all places, she chose to confront him, **here**?*

"Erin," Reuben was amazed his voice sounded cool and unruffled.

"Ben," she replied just as calmly.

Erin was the only person who called him Ben, and he had never cared for the diminutive. It nettled him that she assumed it was okay to use it now... thirty-odd years after...

he forced his irritation aside and focused on his wife. He was pleased to note her accent, which used to send little thrills down his spine, did nothing, didn't even annoy him.

"Was there something you wanted? Would you like me to sign a book maybe?" His accompanying smile was faintly mocking.

"The only thing I want you to sign are the divorce papers." She rejoined, sharply, then he heard her suck in a breath.

"Which I shall be only happy to do, once my lawyers have received, perused, and either agreed with, or countered them. Why are you here, Erin? You made it very clear you wanted no contact with me whatsoever thirty-four years ago. Am I supposed to feel flattered you deigned to come and see me?" Reuben delivered this remark with no inflection at all, and his gaze held no warmth. He leaned back in his chair and, steepling his fingers together, studied her impassively.

Erin Faulkner was taken aback by Reuben's bland indifference to her presence. She anticipated anger, hostility, sorrow even, but this cool detachment shook her — it was so... un-Reuben.

The reason Erin wanted this divorce was two-fold. Dean — the man she had been seeing for the past seven years — recently asked her to marry him, which obliged her to confess she had never divorced her first husband. Secondly, the minute Dean became aware she was still married, he mentioned, in what sounded like nothing more than an afterthought, she ought to be entitled to some recompense. Although Erin was honest enough to admit it was she who walked out, the thought of getting Reuben to pay up was too good to ignore.

Then, two days ago, she saw the poster advertising his

upcoming signing at The Bookshelf. Erin vacillated over whether to attend. She had a copy of his book, of course she did, how could she not? Reuben had a brilliant mind, that was never in question whatever else had broken between them, and she had no doubt anything he published would be outstanding.

His photo on the inside of the rear cover — his friendly open smile, his unruly hair and the laugh-lines at the corners of his beautiful eyes — revived something she believed had fizzled out decades ago. Even knowing she could not expect a welcome, Erin was possessed with the urge to see Reuben again, to find out whether that sensation would be repeated when they came face to face. Moreover, because her lawyer had warned against any kind of meeting — public or private — her contrary mind wanted to do precisely what she shouldn't.

Thirty-four years, an ocean, a continent, and her choices had kept them apart. Now, the only thing separating them was a table, and Erin had never felt further away.

"I saw the poster. I wondered... perhaps you might like to have a coffee or a drink... for old times' sake." *Really Erin — old times' sake? What the hell is the matter with you?* She blinked and swallowed. "Sorry, that was a stupid thing to say. I just wanted to see you. Is that so hard to believe?"

Reuben gaped at her. The silence stretched out, until Erin wanted to scream.

"Truthfully? Yes," Reuben finally retorted. "What's the point? We have absolutely *nothing* to say to each other. You walked out. You left me with our son, who somehow survived being brought up by a relatively inept single father, and who is awesome, by the way. You vanished, dropped off the face of the planet. I had no clue whether you were alive or dead. You ignored me completely. Eventually, your grandmother, presumably to halt the barrage of calls and letters, assured me you *were* alive and well, then took gleeful delight in delivering the final blow. You wanted no more to do with me, with us. Why in heaven's name would I agree to spend one minute with you, much less a cosy chat over a drink?"

Reuben paused and, closing his eyes, waited until his indignation faded. Opening them again, he added, "It's nice to see you, Erin. I am glad you are well and, rest assured, the divorce papers will be signed in a timely manner, once my lawyers are satisfied the terms are reasonable. You must excuse me; I have somewhere I need to be."

Erin experienced a flick of anger. He was calling the shots, that wasn't how it was supposed to go. She had always been the one with the power in their relationship, Reuben was so biddable. A smile, or a kiss and he was putty in her hands. Erin didn't like this self-possessed side to him — at all. She remembered what her lawyer said; she was eligible to receive a substantial payout from Professor Reuben Faulkner. She acknowledged it would have been lovely had Reuben been amenable to a quiet drink. Maybe she could have persuaded him into dinner and then... the idea of one more night of sex with Reuben appealed, it would close the circle nicely. That said, the money was far more tempting than trying to trick her husband into the sack, only to have him use it to reduce her remuneration.

She stared at him for what felt like a lifetime, he didn't flinch, neither did he break eye contact. She was about to walk away, when Reuben spoke again, his tone measured.

"I was angry with you for so long. You have absolutely no idea what your leaving did to us. I had to begin again. I had to learn to live, to breathe without you. I know you struggled to settle, but your behaviour was reprehensible. Then, after all this time, when the only communication was a soulless letter from your solicitors demanding a divorce and a settlement, you waltz in here and assume I will drop everything to have a drink with you." He shook his head. "Did you intend to suggest dinner after we had drinks, and then maybe propose joining me for a nightcap? Was this a set up by your legal rep to dupe me into agreeing to a larger payout?"

"No, no, Ben... come on, I would never..." Erin managed to sound indignant at his suggestion, but his words hit too close to home and the tell-tale pink creeping up her cheeks gave her away.

"Right, of course you wouldn't. Well, now you'll have to inform them your plan was unsuccessful." He rose from his seat and walked over to where Joel and Paige were standing, and the three began packing everything away.

Erin watched them for a moment, noticing the strikingly pretty woman helping Reuben. Her eyes slit, maybe she could get some leverage. What was Reuben's connection to her? There did not seem to be anything even vaguely lover-like in their interaction, or their body-language, but it might prove useful. Erin smiled to herself and left, her spiky heels clicking on the wooden floor.

8
***

Reuben heard the bell over the door chime signalling Erin's retreat, and heaved a sigh of relief. His stomach was knotted from trying to remain unperturbed. Never did he imagine she would turn up out of the blue to a signing, it was too public.

"You okay, Reuben?" Paige asked, quietly.

"Thank you, Paige, yes, funnily enough I am. I suppose meeting Erin here should not seem so implausible, although I hoped we could avoid it. I have no idea what is going on in her head. She seemed to think I would just drop everything and go out for a drink with her. She must be out of her tree." He shook his head again, confounded by her appearance and their subsequent conversation.

"Do you want to go back to your hotel? We can finish up here," Paige offered.

"No, she's gone, and I doubt I'll see her again. Come on, let's get this sorted. Then, if neither of you has plans, I'm treating you to dinner, preferably somewhere they serve wine. An evening with friends is just what this professor ordered!" He winked and grinned, his usual nonchalance returning.

Paige relaxed and grinned back. 'You're on."

"Joel?" Reuben quizzed.

"If you're sure, sir, I'd love to. Better than going home to a cold apartment in the middle of February." He grimaced, and the other two chuckled.

"You don't know anything about cold weather," Paige interjected. "Today was warmer than summer in the UK."

Joel raised a sceptical brow at Reuben, who nodded.

"'Fraid she's right, Joel so, suck it up." His unexpected use of slang made Joel and Paige laugh all the more and, while Reuben dropped those books which didn't sell into their assigned box, the other two folded the table and carried it out to Joel's van.

Half an hour later — after thanking Mr Mullins, the owner of The Bookshelf for his generosity in hosting the signing — the three were ensconced around a table in the dining room of the hotel where Reuben and Paige were staying. It seemed easier than trudging around an area none of them was familiar with — Joel lived outside the centre of the city — trying to find a suitable restaurant.

A bottle of crisp Napa Valley Zinfandel nestled in an ice-bucket, and they were nibbling on a delicious selection of tapas. After the waiter poured the wine, Reuben raised his glass.

"A toast to you both. I could not have managed this book tour without you, either of you. Somehow, you have kept me on time, and more importantly sane." They clinked glasses and sipped the wine. "Here's to the next month."

The evening flew by in a haze of good food, great conversation and a *lot* of laughter. It was the first time they had eaten together. In fact, it was the first time Reuben had seen Paige or Joel outside of a signing and, despite the difference in ages, discovered they shared similar interests. Joel left about nine, confirming he'd see them bright and early the next morning.

Then there were two.

The chat dwindled a little, and in the few moments of quiet, Reuben found himself comparing Paige and Erin. It wasn't really fair to do so, because Paige had never dumped him and fled the country, and he tried not to let that colour his perception. He knew Paige was way too young for him, but she continued to intrigue him. They had spent some part of every day together since arriving in America, yet she might as well have been in London for all the good that did.

Paige had maintained an aloof distance — polite and friendly but nothing more, and rightly so. She was here to do a job, never mind that she could easily be in a committed relationship, hell, she might be married — he had never dared ask. It would shatter his illusion. For Reuben was drawn to Paige Latimer more than any woman he had known, including Erin whom, once, he thought he would love forever.

He yearned to know what her glossy hair would feel like spilling over his hands while he unravelled that immaculate bun. He wanted to trace her shape, slide her out of her tailored suit and adore the body he knew was hidden underneath. Her expressive eyes which were currently shining in the glow from the candles on their table, held him captive, and he hungered to kiss her sensual lips until she begged him to make love to her.

"Reuben...?"

By sheer force of will, he dragged his mind back to the mundane, swallowed and blinked, desperate to banish the picture his brain had just conjured up.

"I do beg your pardon, I missed that. What did you say?"

"I said it was probably time to turn in. We've an early start."

Reuben felt his stomach plummet. This was nothing to do with the busy schedule, it was simply a reaction to knowing Paige was reverting to her professional persona. This evening was like a bubble — a wonderful and very memorable bubble. *Get a grip Reuben,* he admonished silently, *the last thing she needs in her life is some boring old professor who doesn't know when to act his age.*

He plastered a smile on his face and signalled to the waiter. He signed the bill and stood, offering Paige his arm. "Allow me to escort you to your room." He held her gaze, spying an odd flicker in her eyes. There was an almost imperceptible hesitation, then she said.

"Why thank you, kind sir. How gallant." She dipped a pert curtsy and, picking up her tote bag, slipped her arm through his, her fingers curling around his sleeve.

To Reuben it felt like a brand. A kind of effervescence snaked up his forearm at the same time as desire for the woman walking alongside him pulsed through his body.

Bloody hell.

Unbeknownst to Reuben, Paige was beset by a similar swathe of emotions. The last month had been torture. He was seldom more than ten steps away from her during the day, and it was all she could do not to drag him off whatever platform he was speaking from, and demand he kiss her. She *really* wanted to know what his kiss would feel like, what his touch would feel like.

She dreamt of him far too often. It was always the same, they were lying on colourful blanket, on a secluded beach, protected from the glaring sun by the shade of an overhanging palm. His astonishing blue-grey eyes held her immobile, while his fingers teased and tormented, and his voice, like a Siren's song, lulled her... seduced her.

Suddenly they were at her door. *How did that happen?* Paige had no recollection of getting in the lift. She fumbled around in her bag for the key card, finding it in the inside pocket. Withdrawing it, she placed it against the mechanism. The tiny light went green and she opened the door.

"Goodnight, Paige," Reuben had yet to relinquish his hold.

"Good night, Reuben. Thank you for a lovely dinner, I haven't enjoyed myself so much in ages.

"It was my pleasure, and I am glad." Gently, he disentangled her hand from his arm, and inclined his head towards her room.

"Would you like a hot drink?" Paige, while cursing her tongue, could not hold back her request, simultaneously blushing fiery red.

"I can think of nothing I would like more, but I don't want to place you in an uncomfortable position.

Paige frowned. "How could you possibly do that? It's just a drink." The image in her head sending a second wave of heat up her cheeks.

"Erin..." He left that dangling. Neither was naive enough to think today was the one and only time Erin would attempt to persuade Reuben to sign away at least half of his assets. "I do not want her to think she can use you as leverage." Unknowingly echoing Erin's thoughts of earlier. "Even something as innocent as a drink would be enough to throw a spanner in the works. However, if you are serious..." he paused and shifted from foot to foot, opening his palms in a vaguely inviting gesture, "...I should like to take you up on that offer once we have left San Francisco. Oh, unless I am treading on another's toes." He arched a quizzical eyebrow, and Paige blew out a breath she hadn't realised she was holding.

"No other toes, and I would like that too," she smiled shyly.

"Goodnight, Ms Latimer."

"Goodnight, Professor Faulkner."

At the very last moment, Reuben leaned close and brushed his mouth against her cheek. Involuntarily, Paige turned her head and their lips met.

9

———

They both jolted backwards and studied the other warily. The hotel hallway was quiet, and Reuben was certain Paige must hear the thud of his heart. One moment became two, and then three, the atmosphere laden with suppressed longing.

"God, Paige, I'm sorry..." Reuben muttered raking his hand through his hair making it wilder than ever. "No, I'm not sorry, but—"

"Shut up, and kiss me," Paige interrupted, wanting this more than worrying about the consequences. She slid one hand around his neck, the other coming to rest on the waistband of his jeans. Paige loved that Reuben was taller than she, that he had to bend, just a little when his mouth descended on hers. His lips were firm and cool, and they moved over hers with exquisite tenderness. With his left hand, Reuben stroked up her jawline to caress her ear, his fingers entangling themselves in her hair, while his right arm curved around her back.

They kissed for what felt like an age and Paige, while impressed Reuben made no attempt to take it further, desperately wanted him to. As she sank deeper into his embrace it came to her that on the scale of one to ten, as first kisses went, this was somewhere around five hundred. Never in her life, had Paige been kissed like this and she hoped it wasn't going to be a one-time only thing. She didn't think Reuben was that kind of guy, but what did she really know about him, other than his wife ran out on him yonks ago. Despite this, her heart told her to repeat her invitation, even as her head told her not to be such an idiot.

While emotion and reason were arguing, Reuben broke their kiss.

Reuben, whose brain had given up trying to make him see sense, made a concerted effort to pull away. Kissing Paige was like nothing he had ever experienced. Her response — a heady blend of innocence and passion, and in complete contrast with her reserved façade — was quickly undermining any self-control he thought he possessed. Regardless, he still had no intention of placing her in an awkward position.

Drawing a ragged breath, he rested his forehead against hers, they were both trembling from the unexpected intensity. "Paige, I have no idea where this is going, where you want it to go, but I want to kiss you until you can't remember your name. Hell, I want to kiss you until the sun forgets to rise, and there are things I dream of doing to your body that I am way too old to be contemplating. That said, I can't put you in between Erin and me, it's unfair. I have no doubt, after today, she will toss a spanner in the works and I do not need it bouncing back and hitting you." He stopped speaking. *Bloody hell, he sounded like a cross between a poet and a dickhead*! He opened his mouth to retract the nonsense spilling from it, only to be forestalled by a gentle finger on his lips.

Paige smiled, "Please don't, Reuben. Don't take it back. I want all of those things too and for heaven's sake you are *not* too old." She knew exactly how old he was, his personal information was in her files. She knew pretty much everything there was to know about Professor Reuben Faulkner, except perhaps his shoe size and his favourite food... no she knew the latter too — Italian, specifically linguine gamberi. The legal firm she worked for were exhaustive in their background checks with everyone involved in a case, you never knew what surprises the opposition might spring on you.

Reuben flushed, "I'm the wrong side of sixty..."

"Oh well that's it then... totally over the hill." She waved her hand nonchalantly and gave him an impish grin. "Reuben, age is a state of mind. You come across as a bloke who thinks he's still in his thirties; utterly responsible, but knows how to have fun, how to enjoy life! Plus..." she paused and tapped her chin, "...that would make you my toy boy. I rather like that idea." Her grin became a wicked chuckle.

"How about we stop overthinking this. You know what? Erin left you with a three-year-old child thirty-odd years ago. She has made no attempt to contact you in all that time. Until recently, she had no clue how Jake has grown up, whether he... whether *either* of you were still alive. So, you never divorced, so what, that doesn't give her the right to make all the demands. Has she led a celibate life? Has she slept around, had long term liaisons, brief affairs? You are the one who has done this by the book. You have nothing to hide or be ashamed of. Jake is great guy, a loyal son and from what I can tell, adoring husband. Yer've drug him up good." She drawled the last sentence, pulling a responding grin from Reuben.

"Stop apologising for daring to have a life. I acknowledge being overt while we're here is probably not the most prudent plan, but after that, you know what I say?"

Reuben raised a brow.

"I say screw her..."

"I'd prefer to sc..." Reuben stopped. He really could not use that language, however old-fashioned that made him, "... you know..." he smiled. Rather shyly, Paige thought, it was an endearing expression and made her want him all the more.

She grazed his lips with hers, then canted her head to study him. "I would prefer that too." Loving how his face lit up at her words. "Okay, why don't we make a plan to see where this is going, once we've brushed San Francisco off our feet?" Paige was astonished at how forward she was being. She generally liked the guy to be the one who made the first move, but she sensed, if she didn't seize the moment, Reuben might be inclined to slip back into his shell.

Something Lydia had mentioned, when they first reviewed the case, popped into Paige's head. It related to the two research assistants who worked for Reuben, some time prior to him hiring Alex. Apparently, both applied for the job because they were on the hunt for a husband. Lydia, wanting to ensure there were no hidden surprises, delved a bit more deeply and discovered Reuben had never shown any romantic interest in either of them. Once he made it clear he was not in the market for a wife, they quit.

In fact, since Erin left, they could find no evidence of Reuben indulging in anything remotely resembling a romantic relationship, not even a fling. To all intents and purposes, he seemed to be a quiet, retiring sort of bloke, happiest either lecturing, or buried in his research in that gorgeous village in North Yorkshire.

These qualities appealed to Paige. Her last partner,

Ethan, was very outgoing... as she was sure his string of women could attest. He preferred night clubs, bar hopping and sporting events — the code didn't matter, as long as he could place a bet — to a day exploring a stately home or wandering the halls of a museum or art gallery, or just curling up with a book. He considered Paige's love of reading a huge joke. Ethan had not read a single book since he left school; a fact of which he was very proud. When she looked back on it, *that* should have been the giveaway.

All this ran through her mind, while she watched Reuben process her words.

Would he be willing to take a risk?

10

The last three days had been busy with lectures and bookshop appearances. Tomorrow Reuben would be leaving San Francisco, and he was counting the hours. He hadn't heard from Erin following their encounter at The Bookshelf. Curiously, however, since that afternoon he could not shake the sensation he was being watched. He had not caught anyone in the act, but Reuben was not given to fanciful notions and always trusted his instinct. He doubted it was Erin herself, more likely someone from the law firm she had hired, trying to gather whatever dirt they could. He rang Lydia to apprise her of this possible development, and she didn't sound surprised.

"Typical tactic," she said airily, when Reuben concluded his rather convoluted explanation. "We are doing the same. I would be more astonished if they *didn't* have someone tailing you."

"I find it hard to believe my divorce warrants such scrutiny," Reuben grumbled.

"Oh, upping the ante is par for the course," Lydia replied. "They sent us a draft settlement which we red-lined and returned. Pretty sure this will be a result of that."

"I just want this finished. I am not comfortable tiptoeing around, worrying about what I say, and who I say it to. Did Paige tell you about what happened the other day?"

"Yes, she emailed me, but did not overhear the whole conversation. Was there anything pertinent?"

Reuben provided Lydia with a blow-by-blow account of his discussion with Erin. "I reckon she is after at least half. Quite frankly had she not turned up at the signing I might have been amenable, but that irked me. It was as though..." he hesitated, considering his words, then going for full disclosure, "...Erin was trying to see whether she could still get me to give in and agree to whatever she wanted, without argument. Whether she could click her fingers, and I would fall into her arms or, more likely, her bed, because that would muddy the waters sufficiently enough for her to think she could take advantage. I don't think she understands, just because I have a best-selling book, doesn't mean I have become 'someone'," Reuben paused then added, "she seems to think I'm rolling in it."

"Don't worry Reuben, leave us to deal with it. Carry on with your signings and enjoy the rest of your time in the States. Try to get in some sightseeing, Paige tells me you have hardly seen anything.

"Bit pointless going on my own."

"Take Paige, she's never been to America before. I bet she'd love to play tourist."

"I might do that. I know she's been working long hours too."

They chattered for a few more minutes then hung up.

Little did she know, Lydia had, unwittingly, played right into Erin's hands.

. . .

The days whizzed by until, finally, the longest leg of the tour began to wind up. The team had spent almost two weeks in California and all the indications were, it had been worth the extra time. Joel assured Reuben the publishing company, who had received several requests for the latter to return, were thrilled with the response.

Reuben admitted he couldn't decide which he had enjoyed more, the universities or the bookshops. Each venue brought a diverse audience, with an equally diverse selection of questions. They certainly kept Reuben on his toes, but he relished the challenge.

Of Paige, Reuben had seen little. A snatched kiss here and there, a quick squeeze of hands had to suffice. Regardless of their mutual desires, Reuben was so busy he barely managed to eat dinner before falling into bed, and Paige — the time difference meaning she needed to play catch up — often worked until late into the evening.

Memory of that night teased at Reuben, but he didn't want to rush into anything neither of them was ready for. Although, after a thirty-four-year hiatus, it was likely he was as ready as he was ever going to be. It was more he worried, despite what Paige had said the night they first kissed, whether he was being an idiot thinking anyone in their right mind, would be interested in dating — or would that be courting? — an ageing lecturer.

Since leaving San Francisco, Reuben had dismissed that unexplained prickle of warning as a simple overreaction to Erin's appearance. Now, he just wanted to get back to England where they could explore the possibility of a maybe.

In the meantime, Erin was setting a trap, one she considered to be cunning and incontrovertible. Once set in motion, she expected Reuben to capitulate and agree to whatever her attorney demanded, in a bid to prevent the details becoming public. That the consequences could be devastating never crossed her mind.

As luck would have it, Dean, who had fewer scruples than his fiancée, was a technical wizard. At Erin's behest, he had scoured the website of the university where Reuben used to work, finding several images which he had doctored to create a different picture altogether. The alterations would not hold up to close inspection, but a quick glance was usually all that was needed. People believed anything if it was accompanied by a credible statement.

Reuben was not famous enough to trigger much negative press, but he was a well-respected professor, and his book had catapulted him into the public eye. A slur on a, thus far, unblemished reputation could do untold damage for further book deals. A few more compromising photographs, and Erin was certain her soon-to-be ex-husband would crumble under pressure and give her anything she wanted.

All she had to do was plant the seeds of doubt.

Wise to how exhausting book tours can be, Reuben's publishers had organised a week's break in his schedule which was slotted, conveniently, between his last lecture in Los Angeles and his first in Denver. A few days before it was due to begin, Reuben and Paige were strolling back to the hotel after a bookshop signing.

With a mind to Lydia's comments, Reuben — somewhat tentatively — asked Paige whether she might like to join him on a road trip to Denver. He wanted to visit the Grand Canyon and one or two other places on the route, and this seemed the most interesting way to accomplish it.

"We get to be tourists for a while. Plus, this might be the ideal opportunity to see whether what we think is happening, is, or whether it's just our imagination! Not that I think... that is... I don't mean..." Reuben dried up. *Honestly, he was rubbish at this.*

Paige chuckled. "Thank you, Reuben. That sounds wonderful and very exciting. I love road trips."

Reuben couldn't hide his relief. "Great, and I think fly-drive would be the best plan. Fly to Vegas then hire a car and drive from there. Joel told me there's a fantastic resort... hmm... the Grand Hotel, which is apparently just outside the entrance to the national park. I had a look on the map and, as well as the obvious, there's plenty of places to explore."

"Have you been to the Grand Canyon?" Paige asked curiously, knowing this wasn't Reuben's first trip to America.

"No, funnily enough I haven't. I've seen a bit of California but, for the most part, we tended to stay in and around San Francisco when I came with Erin. It was more visiting her family than doing any real travelling. I kept on at her to..." He stopped abruptly. "Sorry, that was insensitive and inappropriate. You don't need to know my decades-old holiday arguments."

"Don't stress, Reuben." Paige waved her hand, airily. "This is bound to happen. We both have our fair share of baggage. If this is going to become what I hope it is, we're going to need to be comfortable sharing the crap we've been through."

Reuben heard the 'what I hope it is,' and felt a smile

curve his lips. "You're right, Paige, and me too." He pulled her close for a quick kiss which became rather longer, the pair quickly forgetting the world around them.

Neither was aware of a figure lurking in the bushes at the opposite side of the street, snapping several photos. The man behind the lens was amassing quite the collection of interesting pictures. It had been worth the cost of the trip down to LA. Erin would be very grateful and she always knew how to demonstrate her appreciation.

11

Mid-afternoon, four days later, Reuben and Paige were pulling into the entrance of the Grand Hotel. The journey had been relaxed and the roads quiet, it being low season for holidaymakers. The comfortable sedan Reuben hired at McCarran Airport in Las Vegas, ate up the miles. Alighting from the car, the first thing to strike them was the crisp, dry air. Cold enough for their breath to form miniscule white clouds when they spoke.

"Goodness, I'm glad we brought winter gear." Paige shivered, while she reached into the back seat, to grab her jacket. Shrugging into it, she added. "Brrr... now I need hot chocolate, or mulled wine, or both... yes, definitely, both."

"Yeah, but if we're daft enough to come in February, what can we expect." Reuben grinned. "Mind, it makes for great photography weather, and look at that sky — amazing." The sun was on its downward journey. Above them the sky was still a bright azure, but at the horizon it was a much darker hue, heralding the sunset. "Joel said one of the best things, is to get up early and watch the sunrise over the canyon. It'll be chilly, but I reckon it would be worth it."

"I'm game," Paige replied, gladly taking Reuben's prof-

fered hand as they walked into the hotel. An hour thereafter
— checked in, car parked, and bags unpacked — they were
enjoying a glass of red wine in the Canyon Star Saloon.
Following a mouth-watering steak dinner, the couple spent
the rest of the evening poring over a guidebook, debating
what to do. The forecast for the week was reasonable, but
the concierge explained the national park was subject to
storms with minimal warning, so it was best to plan accord-
ingly. He also mentioned the north rim was closed for the
winter season.

By the time Reuben and Paige were making their way to
their adjacent rooms, they had decided on several places
they wanted to explore during their stay. On Joel's advice,
Reuben had purchased a park pass, online, which allowed
them to access the park whenever they wanted.

"So, are you coming to watch the sunrise?" Reuben
asked when they reached Paige's door.

"Of course, wouldn't miss it."

"Sleep well." He leaned in and brushed his lips to hers.

"I'm sure I will," she murmured, sliding her hands up
and around Reuben's neck, drawing him closer. "I just need
to..." She kissed him, with sublime deliberation, gratified
when she heard the muffled hiss of his sigh and felt his
heart rate increase. His arms encircled her, moulding her
against him.

After long moments, Reuben lifted his head and
muttered in an unsteady voice. "We'd better stop now,
before I can't." He did not loosen his embrace.

"We don't actually have to. We are adults." Paige rested
her forehead against Reuben's, relishing this moment.

"I know..." he paused, then added with a hint of diffidence,
"Paige, I'm out of practice at this, so please bear with me. Yes, I
want to make love to you, of course I do. You're a beautiful

woman with a body that could stop traffic. Thing is, I'm a bit old-school. I don't want to jump into bed at the first opportunity. That says little for my ability to think with anything other than my dick... if you'll pardon the expression. I want to court you, to get to know you on a more personal level. I want to discover your likes and dislikes, what makes you smile and gives you joy as well as what hurts and saddens you. I want to do all this, before everything becomes mired by sex. I want to know your mind before I steal your body... and trust me, I can think of nothing I'd rather do than steal your body."

Reuben flushed, unsure whether he was making any sense, or it sounded as though he was prevaricating. He started to speak again, but Paige, as was becoming a habit, pressed a light finger to his lips.

"You are better at this, than you think, and I agree. I like the idea of being courted, sounds very romantic."

Reuben smiled, a gentle — and for Paige, toe-curling — smile before sweeping an exaggerated bow. "My lady. Now, time to sleep, we've got to be awake at silly o'clock in the morning. I'll give you a knock when I'm ready."

Okay, thanks." Paige grinned. She pressed the card against the little box next to the handle and, hearing the click, pushed open the door. "Night."

"Night." Reuben waited until her door was closed, then took three strides to his own room. Once inside he went over to the desk, which stood against the wall opposite the bed. Placing his hands, palms flat, on the surface, he bent his head and strove for calm. Paige was like a drug; the feel of her in his arms, the taste of her on his lips was intoxicating. Reuben shook his head, acknowledging his behaviour was more akin to that of a gawky adolescent than a man nearing retirement, but his response to Paige was like nothing he'd ever felt before. Not even with Erin, with whom — until very recently — he presumed he was still in love.

He switched on the television for a few minutes, while he got ready for bed, in the hope it distracted him from his baser urges. It didn't, and it was well after midnight before he finally fell asleep.

Six-thirty the next morning, saw Reuben and Paige pulling into a parking spot at Navajo Point, the highest elevation along the south rim. There were already a few other hardy souls who had picked their vantage point. It was bitterly cold, and frost coated the ground. The air was crystal clear, the shifting gloom of the pre-dawn throwing all manner of interesting shadows and shapes along the canyon wall.

Scouting out a good position, Reuben and Paige exchanged quiet greetings with those around them. They joined in the good-natured banter about getting up so early, and how far some had travelled to witness this marvel of nature. One or two people, standing nearby remarked that it was like watching the rebirth of the world.

Before long, the sky began its ceaseless ritual, morphing from subdued greys, to plum and amethyst, threaded with traces of delicate fuscia, and trimmed with indigo. As the ball of flame peeked over the horizon, turquoise streaks pushed through, the promise of a perfect winter's day.

Reuben and Paige were transfixed. There were several moments of absolute silence, not even the click of a camera could be heard, while the audience watched one of Earth's most spectacular displays unfold. The sun rose over the canyon, fingers of amber fire caressing the various layers which ran like ribbons along the contours of the steep, rocky sides. The constantly changing hues reminiscent of restless rivers searching for the sea.

Then as one, the sound of camera shutters undulated like a wave along the watchers, followed by murmured conversations about the awe-inspiring scene in front of them. Reuben and Paige didn't speak, to do so, felt... irreverent, although both snapped numerous pictures.

The dramatic splendour of the seemingly endless vista, with its craggy rock formations and sparse yet tenacious flora, softened by the dusting of white — made Reuben ponder the existence of a celestial architect. For how could such beauty be random?

As the dawn yielded to full daylight, the atmosphere changed. Laughter and chatter filled the air, while those people who had driven up in RVs began to make breakfast and brew coffee. The smell of frying bacon set Reuben's stomach growling, and he suggested they return to the hotel for breakfast.

"We can come back again later. I reckon it would be fun to park and ride. I think the orange bus goes to the best viewpoints."

"Sounds like a plan. Come on, I'm cold and famished." Paige tucked her arm through Reuben's and the couple strolled back to the car.

12

———

By mid-morning, they were back. It was already bustling with visitors, but they found a parking spot relatively easily, and only had to wait five minutes for the bus. Both thoroughly enjoyed the tour, Paige introducing Reuben to the fun of 'selfies' against the backdrop of the canyon. After an overdue coffee, Reuben asked whether Paige was interested in the Skywalk. She declined with a shudder.

"Thank you, but no. I know people rave about it, but I cannot bring myself to walk out onto a glass horseshoe sticking out over an abyss. I would freak out. The views we've already seen are enough for me but hey, don't let me stop you going, if you fancy it."

Reuben grinned. "I have no desire to venture onto it either. I just didn't want you to miss out on any of the Grand Canyon experience."

Paige nudged him in the shoulder, and the two stood for a moment chatting about where to have lunch and what to do for the remainder of the day. So engrossed were they, neither registered the approach of a young couple.

. . .

"Well, fancy meeting you here," an amused voice broke into Reuben and Paige's conversation. Reuben spun around and came face to face with his son. His jaw dropped.

"Jake?" Reuben's gaze travelled to the woman standing alongside Jake. "*Alex*? How in the world...?" His stupefied tone made the new arrivals laugh.

"We fancied a holiday to celebrate our wedding anniversary and to cut a veeeeery long and convoluted story short, I managed to persuade someone called Joel to tell us where you were." Jake explained.

"You *fancied* a holiday?" Reuben narrowed his eyes, suspiciously. "That does not sound like either of you, and I know the US is not on your list of drop everything and visit places."

"Awww, Dad, we wanted to surprise you."

Alex intervened. "Okay, I admit it, we were worried especially when you mentioned Erin had turned up. We both needed a break, it *is* our anniversary, and a week here is *almost* as good as a week in Rome." She grinned mischievously at her father-in-law. "Plus," she waved her hand towards the canyon's rim, "this is extraordinary, I'm so glad we came. Hi Paige," she added belatedly with a cheerful smile.

"Hi, Alex," Paige responded in kind, and then squeaked when, unexpectedly, she was drawn into a hug.

"Glad you're both here." Reuben hugged Alex then went to shake hands with his son.

"It's been nearly two months, Dad, that's about the longest we've gone without seeing each other. I think a hug is in order for your favourite son," Jake bantered.

"Humph," was Reuben's considered response but he did not fight Jake's bear hug, groaning when his son planted a smacker right on his mouth. "Ewww... watch it... that's pushing your luck, Jake. You can quickly become my most annoying son, you know."

Laughing and completely unrepentant, Jake stepped away from his father, and drew Alex against him. The group fell to enthusiastic gossiping about what they had been doing since they last saw each other.

Not one of the four, noticed a man, rugged up in expensive winter hiking gear, snapping photos of the area. As was his intent, he blended in with the rest of the tourists milling about. His efforts to get just the right image had been frustrated until five minutes ago. Checking to ensure the photo he had was clear, he smiled with satisfaction.

Excellent!

The subsequent week was one, which Reuben and Paige looked back on as being idyllic. Although cold, the days were wreathed in sunshine. The nights were frigid, but clear skies offered the chance to stargaze — the heavens full to bursting with millions of tiny pinpricks of light, and it became a game to try to spot the constellations.

Paige was astounded. Living most of her life in London, she rarely saw the stars because they tended to be obscured by light pollution from the city. Plus, it wasn't something she had thought about, prior to this holiday. The other three, who came from a tiny village, with little street lighting — while riveted by the sheer expanse of the night sky and the abundance of stars — were less astonished. Such spectacles were a regular occurrence.

Reuben did indeed court Paige. Despite his own lack of confidence in matters of the heart, he made Paige feel like the most adored woman on the planet. Attentive without being obsequious, and affectionate without taking their intimacy beyond a kiss — all be they many and fervent. Paige felt like the heroine of a period romance novel, and she relished Reuben's courtesy.

While exploring the Grand Canyon and surrounding sights — sometimes with Jake and Alex, sometimes on their own — Reuben and Paige talked about everything under the sun, discovering they had plenty in common. There was a lot of laughter, a lot of ribbing and, inevitably, the occasional mild disagreement. As the days ticked by, each realised they found the other more interesting the longer they spent together, acknowledging — so far only to themselves — the kernel of attraction was blossoming into something profound and enduring.

The holiday was coming to an end. Reuben's commitments in Denver loomed and, although the ten-hour drive would be comfortable in the hire car, he and Paige had decided to break the journey and have a night at Grand Junction.

It had been a fun week, the four had fallen into a loose routine of meeting up over breakfast, separating to do their own thing for most of the day, then coming together again for drinks in the hotel bar, before dinner. Jake and Alex treated Paige as though they had known her forever, to Reuben's well-concealed delight.

The evening prior to their departure, Alex and Reuben were following Jake and Paige out of the restaurant, when Alex murmured, "What did I say to you not so long ago about dating?"

Reuben grinned sheepishly and could not prevent his cheeks reddening. "Early days, Alex. Early days."

"But you really like her, don't you?"

"I do, but I don't want to rush things. I've been out of this game a long time, and am not some young..."

"Oh pooh," Alex interrupted, "don't be such a worry wort. You're not giving Paige much credit, are you?" She twisted to face her father-in-law, who raised a quizzical brow. "Reuben, Paige isn't some giddy girl, neither is she Tricia or whatshername... Jill was it? Anyway, if Paige was after some rich husband to gad about the world with, she wouldn't be hanging around with you. No, let me finish..." when Reuben tried to interject, "...she's seeing you at your most vulnerable. She's not daft, she knows exactly how crappy divorces can become, yet she's here. Paige came with you, when she could easily have gone on ahead with Joel and met you in Denver. Please don't miss out on this because you're afraid to take a chance."

"I'm not afraid."

"Aren't you?"

Reuben opened his mouth to reject Alex's challenge, when he paused. "Okay, maybe just a little. Falling in love is scary when you're my age."

"Falling in love? Oh, Reuben." Alex clasped her hands to her chest and feigned a swoon, "how romantic."

"Alex, don't you go all gooey on me. I haven't even told Paige yet, so no spilling the beans, and *please* don't say anything to Jake until after tomorrow. I don't need him winding me up."

"I promise, if you promise me, you'll tell her soon. She deserves to know, and I guarantee she feels the same way.

You two don't see what outsiders see..." she kissed Reuben's cheek, "...now, time for a nightcap, I think."

No more was said, and the remainder of the evening was taken up with gossip about the next leg of Reuben's tour.

The following morning, after a flurry of goodbyes, the two couples went their separate ways. Alex and Jake were heading to Las Vegas to return their hire car, before returning home via New York. Reuben and Paige set out for Grand Junction.

13

Regrettably, two days later, when Reuben and Paige arrived in Denver, their happy bubble burst and, if not for a sharp eye, Erin's greed might have ruined everything. After checking in at the hotel, Reuben's phone — which he disliked having to carry at the best of times and so had turned it off for most of the previous week — rang.

It was Lydia.

"Reuben, where have you been, and why was your phone off? Check your email." Lydia sounded tense, nothing like her usual unflappable self.

"What's going on Lydia?" Reuben asked.

"Check your email, then we'll talk." Abruptly, she hung up.

Reuben stared at his phone in puzzlement. He felt like a child being chastised for playing up in class.

"What's her problem?" he muttered.

"Something wrong?" Paige questioned, wheeling her suitcase over to where he was standing in the middle of the atrium.

"Not a single clue," Reuben rejoined, "but your boss did not seem happy, maybe she hasn't had her coffee yet." He glanced at his watch trying to work out the time difference. "No wait, that can't be right, it's... what almost eight-thirty in the evening in London."

"Wow, that's late, even for Lydia. What did she say?"

"She growled at me for not having my phone on, then told me to check my email." While they were standing, Reuben's phone pinged several times. He glanced at his screen, there were at least ten text messages and almost double that in missed calls. "What the hell?" He showed Paige the screen.

"Bugger," Paige frowned, "that's odd, why didn't she call me when she couldn't get you?"

"No idea. Let's find our rooms and get sorted. Then, if you're happy to come to my room, I'll log on. I want you to see whatever she's sent me."

"Good plan."

They located Paige's room first.

"Just pop along when you're ready. I'm number 1318," Reuben said as she wheeled her suitcase through the door.

"Give me five minutes." She grinned.

After dumping her bags, and using the bathroom, Paige tracked Reuben to his room, which turned out to be a suite and very swanky, at the far end of the corridor. Answering Paige's quiet knock, Reuben led her over to a small sofa, positioned under the window and next to a coffee table — on which his laptop was powering up. Thankfully, he was able to connect to the wi-fi without a problem and, upon opening his email, Reuben was surprised to see a swathe of messages, all from Lydia.

He clicked on the earliest.

Reuben, please call as soon as you read this, we have a problem.

The others were much the same, although Lydia's language indicated she was becoming increasingly annoyed with his lack of response. The last one went into more detail and there was a collection of images attached.

Reuben studied them, gaped, rubbed his eyes and looked again. *What the hell?* He picked up his phone and dialled Lydia's direct line. When she answered, he put it on speaker. He wanted Paige to hear this too.

"You've seen them, talk to me." Lydia didn't give Reuben chance to speak, launching into a tirade about hiding relevant information. Information which could give Erin everything she wanted, information, which could easily ruin him if his publishers found out, not to mention his university where he still held privileges.

"Wait, Lydia, back the truck up. I have never seen these pictures before. I have no recollection of them being taken."

"I don't imagine you were supposed to *know* they were being taken, Reuben, that's the point. Erin's lawyer is threatening to expose you as some kind of sleaze, and the reason Erin left was because you were consistently involved in clandestine relationships with students, of both sexes, who were not necessarily of age, before, during, and after your marriage. This is what we call going for the jugular. I told you they would exploit the slightest detail."

While Lydia was speaking, all colour had drained from Reuben's face. "But I haven't. I never..." He couldn't continue. That his wife would stoop to this, shocked and appalled him. He stared at the images and shook his head. The backgrounds were varied but in several, he recognised the gardens at the university where he had worked for almost thirty years, where he still gave the occasional lecture. Some were faded, some less so, and purported to be a selection of photos collated over an extended period. This seemed peculiar to him. Who could be bothered to stalk someone for that long, without contacting him at all? Why wait decades? Blackmail was an ugly word, but it whispered at the corner of his mind.

Reuben found his voice. "Okay, firstly, the mere fact you suspect I could, I *would* be involved in such reprehensible behaviour means you possess an extremely low opinion of me. Secondly, I have never had *any* kind of relationship with a student, not then, not now. Erin was not a student when we met, she was visiting a friend whose husband worked at the uni. Thirdly, and as I've said before, I'm not interesting enough to engender this kind of scrutiny, something is badly wrong here. Lastly, since I know I'm innocent of what she's implying, there has to be something hinky about these photos. Can you give me a couple of hours, or would you rather wait 'til morning?"

There was a long-suffering sigh from the other end of the line. "Hinky? Kinky more like. No, I would not rather wait until the morning, we're already behind the eight ball. Two hours, then I'm calling back. Is Paige with you?"

"Yes, I'm here, Lydia," Paige spoke up.

"I need you to take control and, if you need to run interference, do so. This cannot be leaked."

"Lydia," Reuben interjected, "Seriously, Erin's just doing this to force a settlement. No one else cares."

"Don't be so naive, Reuben," Lydia hissed. "You are on an international book tour and, while your celebrity maybe minor compared with most, you have become a household name, which is not solely restricted to the academic community. Furthermore, Erin's lawyers don't actually need to publish these images, the mere suggestion they will, is enough to grab our attention. I warned you about skeletons and mud."

"And I told you everything." Reuben's temper was fraying. "I don't have any skeletons, or dusty closets or reasons for anyone to fling mud. I presume you've spoken to all those people who offered to vouch for my character. Surely if a single one of them was suspicious, they would have mentioned it. Erin left me, without warning. Goddammit, Lydia, we made love that night, and as soon as I was asleep, she crept out of the house like a bloody thief. What sort of person does that? She walked away from our son without a backward glance and refused to acknowledge my existence. Now she thinks she can... wait..."

Reuben hesitated, a number of oddities striking him. He voiced them. "Why now? After all this time, why now? If she's had these pictures for so long, who took them? Why did they take them? What prompted her to, apparently, engage someone to follow me on the off chance of capturing me in a compromising position, when she wasn't even in the country? If she thought I was screwing around, let alone with anyone underage..." he paused as a wave a nausea roiled through him, "...why did she stay with me? Why didn't she disclose my apparent philandering to the authorities then? Why did she sleep with me? Without being too explicit, she'd have to be a damn good actress to fake her reactions. Why did she continue to have sex with me if she thought I was doing what I'm being accused of?"

Paige, who was examining the images, caught Reuben's arm. "Lydia, excuse me for cutting in, but please can you give us those two hours? I think I have something here."

There was a grumbled agreement. "Two hours, no more."

"Thank you..." and before either Reuben or Lydia could

argue, Paige pressed the red icon on Reuben's phone, ending the call.

"What have you got?" Reuben asked, perplexed.

"Okay, I've downloaded the images, so we can see them full screen. I'm going to scroll through them, and I want you to tell me what you see."

Paige opened the first picture. It showed Reuben embracing a younger woman. She was kissing his cheek. The background could have been a park or a large garden.

"It's me hugging a woman in a garden. It looks pretty innocent to be honest."

"Next one."

In the second image, Reuben was the one being kissed — on the mouth, but this time by a man. It had been taken with a telephoto lens; the grin on Reuben's face and the affection in his eyes, undeniable. Despite some similarities in the style of the pair's attire — both were wearing outdoor gear, the unidentified man, who was facing away from the camera, appeared to be much younger than Reuben.

Reuben's brow creased in puzzlement. "Next one," he requested. It showed him with a young girl. Like the previous image, she had her back to the photographer, but it was obvious she was wearing a skimpy outfit. Reuben frowned, swallowing quickly, hoping he wasn't about to vomit. "Keep going," he instructed, tersely.

Paige scrolled through them all.

None of the people he was pictured with were recognisable, because in each shot, they faced away from the camera. All the backgrounds were a bit blurry, possibly deliberately.

How much worse could it get?

14

Reuben was floored, and when the last image slid up the screen, he bowed his head. He felt like someone had scoured his insides with a metal brush. He could not get his brain around why anyone would do this. *Erin*. Her face swam over his vision and an anger greater than anything he had experienced before, engulfed him. He knew he was innocent, but photographic evidence was hard to disprove.

He lifted a defeated gaze to Paige. "If I wasn't seeing this with my own eyes, I would not believe it, but how can I refute any of these pictures? I have no leg to stand on. I'm done, it's over. I'll tell Lydia to give Erin whatever she wants. Praise the Lord, Moorview is in Jake's name. I'm sorry, Paige, you don't deserve to be dragged into this shitfest. Maybe you ought to go back to London. The last thing you need is to have your name associated with me. It'll probably backfire on the firm, and that's not fair, especially when Mr Tomlinson was generous enough to take my case because of his connection to Alex." He stood up.

Then Paige shocked him.

"Sit your damn cute butt back down, mister."

"I beg your pardon?" He gawked at her.

"Sorry, *Professor*, and you heard." She grinned, unrepentantly. "I asked you to really look at these pictures. You are only seeing what Erin's lawyers want you, want other people to see. Take a few moments, study them closely. There is something about every single one which renders Erin's accusations impossible. Ready?"

Reuben nodded and, after lowering himself back onto the sofa, did as Paige requested.

He spent ages inspecting each image; scrutinising the background the figures in the foreground, their clothing, hair colour — everything. Didn't matter how long he looked; Reuben simply could not figure out to what Paige alluded.

"I give up," he sighed an hour later.

"Men…" Paige threw up her hands. Before Reuben could react, she leaned across and kissed him, soundly, on the lips.

The familiar heat washed through him and, even knowing it was imprudent, he drew her into his arms and reciprocated with searing interest.

Moments passed, then Paige lifted her head, her breathing erratic. "Why, Reuben Faulkner, that was sneaky," she said, her voice a little hoarse.

"Are you complaining?" He smiled, crookedly.

"Nope, but let's sort this first, then we can pick up where we left off." She wriggled out of his embrace and pointed at the screen.

Reuben chuckled, he couldn't help it, despite the gravity of the situation, her excitement was palpable. "Clearly whatever you are bursting to tell me, is way more important than being kissed," he remarked wryly.

Paige shook her head. "Look. Look at *you*, ignore the rest of the image, concentrate on you. Describe what you see?"

The picture was faded, affecting the colours, but Reuben gave it his best shot. "I see a man standing on a path. He's wearing dark trousers, probably jeans or maybe chinos, and a dark jacket over what could be a green or possibly a brown jumper. His shoes look like they could be brogues." He shrugged.

"Ok, yep, I agree with all that. Anything else?"

Reuben studied the image. "Not that I can see... what am I missing."

Paige gave him a triumphant grin. "Look at your hair?"

Flummoxed, Reuben squinted at his head in the picture. Then it dawned on him. "You can see the grey in my hair." He looked again making sure he wasn't imagining things. Then he checked the other pictures. In each one, his hair mirrored how it looked in the previous one.

"Exactly!" Paige crowed. "These cannot have been taken years ago, they must have been taken recently. One more thing. She ran her fingers across the trackpad until she found the one purportedly showing Reuben in an intimate embrace with another man. "This time look at the man you're hugging."

Reuben studied the picture, something about it was niggling at him. The problem was, much as Paige kept reminding him to ignore the background, because it was nowhere he recognised, it was affecting his recall. The identity of the man refused to be pinned down. "Sorry, I feel I ought to know who it is, but..."

"It's your *son!*" Paige couldn't hold back any longer and was almost bouncing in her eagerness to tell him. "It's the day he and Alex surprised us at the Grand Canyon. Someone has doctored the background and made it seem as though it was taken years ago. The woman in the skimpy outfit might actually be Erin, a couple of others might be her too, and I'm pretty sure the women in the rest of the images are either Alex or me. Same thing, the background altered to fool the viewer. If a few *are* Erin, they might well have been taken here in the States, after she walked out, making their authenticity, impossible"

Reuben stared at Paige, then swung his gaze back to the screen and scrolled through. Now he knew what he was looking for, it was obvious. *Bloody, bugger and sod, how could he have been so gullible?*

"Dammit, you're right. Paige you are a bloody genius." Reuben hauled her against him and kissed her with all the pent-up desire he'd been trying so desperately to curb. Paige, who felt she ought to protest — purely for propriety's sake, of course — melted against him, returning his kiss with equal fervour. The gamut of emotions they had both been dealing with, coalesced, quickly spiralling out of control. Hearts thrummed, breathing quickened, and hands — hampered somewhat by clothes — searched, teasing... tantalising... discovering.

Caught up in a whirlwind of passion, everything else faded into the background. Had they not tumbled, ignominiously, off the sofa, it is likely their promise to call Lydia would have gone unfulfilled.

"Oooof... sorry, are you okay?" Reuben asked Paige, now lying underneath her, between the sofa and the table.

Paige giggled. "I'm fine. I feel a bit like a teenager mind... talk about getting carried away. Good job we said we'd call Lydia back, not the other way around." She stretched up and brushed her lips to Reuben's cheek. "Come on, Professor Faulkner, methinks 'tis time we played a little game of our own."

Shortly thereafter, via video chat, they revealed what Paige had unearthed, to Lydia. The lawyer was stunned and affirmed she would send the images to someone called Spencer Harris — their preferred expert. That a legal firm required a *preferred* expert in digital images, was a sad indictment on the levels to which parties would sink in a divorce battle, but Reuben was inordinately glad they had one.

"It'll take Spencer a couple of days to get these processed, I expect. Until then, I think we should keep this to ourselves, while we come up with a game plan. The fewer people know we're onto them, the better. I'll get in touch when we're ready for the next step. Enjoy Denver, but Reuben, please leave your phone on." Lydia's tone was dry.

"You have my word." Reuben grinned; relief etched on his face. They cut the connection and he faced Paige. "This calls for wine, dinner and a large whisky, not necessarily in that order. I do hope you'll join me."

"I would love to. Give me half an hour to shower and change. How about we meet up in the lobby?"

"Great, see you shortly."

Paige left the room, her thoughts churning. Erin's machinations aside, Reuben's spontaneous reaction to her hasty detective work spoke volumes. After what had happened with Ethan, she was more inclined to trust people's behaviour than their words — in her opinion, the instinctive response was the reliable one.

She just hoped her intuition was correct.

15

They had a wonderful meal at an Italian restaurant just off Larimer Square, enjoying perhaps a glass of wine more than was sensible, but they *were* celebrating. Maybe a little tipsy, they decided to stroll around the historic hub, before returning to the hotel. It was a chilly night; the air had a sour edge — a harbinger of snow, a few flakes already beginning to drift down from a laden sky. Reuben slung an arm around Paige, while they meandered, admiring the Victorian buildings and the eclectic mix of cafés, shops, and galleries housed within.

"Brrrr... it's freezing. I need a hot drink." Paige shivered.

"Want to stay and have one around here, or go back to the hotel?"

"Let's go back. I want to take off my shoes, get into my pj's, and curl up on the couch or the bed, watch some telly."

Reuben swallowed before he replied, the image of Paige in pj's doing weird things to his brain. "Okay. I'd like to come back here during the day though, if we have time. It's a fascinating area." His words came out as a croak.

"You okay? Not getting a cold, are you?" Paige enquired, solicitously.

"Nope, all good... just... never mind," he replied, unwilling to admit how profound an effect she had on him.

Paige glanced at Reuben, curiously. He sounded a bit odd. His expression was bland but, as though aware of her gaze, he turned his head to look at her. His arresting grey-blue eyes twinkled, and his mouth curved into a gentle smile. Her heart skittered. Loath to break the moment, she held her tongue and simply snuggled into his shoulder. They were back at the hotel in a matter of minutes. When they reached their floor, and as he did at the end of each evening, Reuben took his sweet time kissing Paige, in the dim alcove at her door.

His control rapidly deserting him, Reuben broke their embrace and said goodnight, giving her hand a light squeeze.

"Want to come in for a night cap?" Paige had no idea what prompted her invitation. She hadn't asked him since their first night at the Grand Canyon; the ball was in his court.

"Yes," Reuben replied baldly, shocking himself. He knew accepting her offer was rash — neither of them was particularly sober, and therefore, sense might well have flown out of the window. For once, Reuben didn't care. He was tired of trying to keep his distance. Yes, his motives were laudable, but chivalry be damned. He saw Paige's eyes widen and grinned, a trifle self-consciously. He bent his head until his mouth grazed her ear. "Yes, please I would love to come in. A night cap sounds like the perfect end to the day."

· · ·

Blushing, Paige unlocked her door. Her room, a smaller version of Reuben's, was warm; the subdued lighting giving it a cosy ambience. Stepping over to the desk on which stood a kettle, she waved her hand towards the sofa. "Grab a seat. I can offer coffee or a variety of teas... hmmm... oh, there's hot chocolate..." She picked up a mug and waited for Reuben's answer, twisting around to look at him when it didn't come. He was standing in the middle of the room, watching her, his expression unreadable. "What's wrong?"

"Nothing, absolutely nothing."

"Then...?" she faltered, perplexed.

In two strides, he closed the gap, and taking the mug from her fingers, replaced it on the tray. Cupping one hand around her nape he kissed her — deeply, slowly, and sensuously. He had kissed her many, *many* times before but, to Paige, this was different, there was something more going on. She felt his other hand slide around her waist coming to rest, fingers splayed, on the dip at the base of her spine.

"R-Reuben," she husked.

"Hush..." He recaptured her mouth, stealing her words, shaping her body to his. Paige — astonished to realise it was actually possible for knees to feel as though they had turned to water — gave up and sank into his embrace.

For Reuben this was it. There was no going back, and if Paige allowed it, he wanted to make love to her... here... tonight... *but*, there was something he wanted to confess first.

He lifted his head.

Paige opened glazed eyes. Her hair was all mussed and her cheeks pink.

"Paige..."

She tilted her head

"I love you." He blurted out the declaration, hectic colour flaring up his face.

There was absolute silence.

Slack jawed, Paige stared at Reuben, stunned.

"I b-beg your p-pardon", she stammered. She shook her head... she was dreaming... she *had* to be dreaming.

"I love you. I can't pretend otherwise. I am head over heels, irrevocably, eternally, recklessly, passionately, irrationally, hopelessly in love with you. If you are game to take a chance on an ageing professor, I will do everything in my power to make you feel loved and adored, and perhaps one day you might feel the same way."

"Reuben..." Paige repeated, her left hand skimming the stubble shadowing his jaw. Their eyes locked, electricity sizzled between them. Paige brushed her lips to his. "I have loved you almost since the moment we met... irrevocably, eternally, recklessly, passionately, irrationally, and hopelessly." She echoed his words and heard him sigh as he reclaimed her lips.

Reuben's fear he had forgotten *how* to make love was allayed... some things, apparently, were instinctual. He refused to rush. This was their first time, and he wanted it to be special. He wanted this to be a night they would remember for the rest of their lives.

Before Paige could stop him — not that there was much likelihood of her doing so — Reuben did what he'd been wanting to do from the day they met... he unpinned her hair. It spilled around her shoulders in a curtain of treacle silk, begging for him to entwine his fingers through it... which, of course, he did, the feel of it against his skin as provocative as her kiss.

Time was suspended... or so it appeared. Initial nerves — being undressed, being seen naked was... daunting, even for Paige whose last relationship was much more recent than Reuben's — were soon banished. Reuben's heated gaze when he divested Paige of the last of her clothes, sent a glissade of delicious tingles all the way down her body, right to her toes, and her shyness fled.

Somehow, they ended up on the bed, although neither could recall how they got there, whereupon, Reuben proceeded to explore every part of Paige. His leisurely seduction was more potent than any aphrodisiac, and he continued to weave his magic, until Paige was writhing underneath him, sparking a firestorm, which quickly consumed her.

...and what a way to go... Paige mused absently, as she surrendered.

Reuben came awake, momentarily confused. The bed was huge, the room unfamiliar and he seemed to have had a rough night. The bedding was tangled, and all the pillows had vanished. He stretched, his toe coming into contact with a leg. Recollection hit. Paige! A wide grin warmed his face and, noticing the clock was showing 6:35... still early... he sought under the rumpled blankets.

He was rewarded by a shocked squeak, then a giggle. A tousled head appeared from beneath the comforter and a pair of ocean-turquoise eyes bore into him.

Paige too, glanced at the clock.

"Reuben Faulkner, how rude, waking me so early. This girl needs her beauty sleep, you know."

"I beg to differ. This girl is the most beautiful I have ever clapped eyes on, but if you want to go back to sleep, I won't stop you." Stroking his fingers lightly up and down her thigh, hearing her breathing stutter.

"Hey, that's not fair." Paige quivered, heat pooling in her core, her heartbeat quickening.

"Who ever said I play fair?"

"Reuben..." She arched into him, whispering his name — an entreaty, a desire, and a future.

16

The next few days were as full as Reuben expected. The various lectures and several signings lined up by his publisher, proved popular for students and non-academics alike, many of whom peppered Reuben with questions about whether he was writing another book. He was happy to reveal he was almost finished an in-depth study of Hadrian's legal and social reforms, which he hoped would be released towards the end of the year.

"...so if you are looking for a Christmas present with a difference," he concluded with a wry grin, making the audience chuckle.

Reuben spent every available spare moment with Paige. They explored Denver and its surrounds, Paige especially wanted to visit Colorado Springs because one of her favourite television shows was set there, and they even managed to fit in two nights in Aspen. The final leg of the tour saw them visit Dallas and Atlanta in quick succession, finishing up in Charlotte.

April was looming; Reuben had been on the road for two months and, California aside, rarely stayed more than a couple of nights in each city. He wanted to unpack his suitcase, wear different clothes, relax in his quiet cottage in Rosedale Abbey — preferably with Paige — and not be expected to talk to strangers for at least a week. On top of this, lurking in the background was the situation with Erin. He definitely wanted *that* resolved sooner rather than later, it was like a millstone around his neck.

During the previous two weeks, Lydia had kept Paige and him abreast of developments. Spencer, the photography expert, affirmed the pictures were faked; good enough to pass muster, or withstand a cursory glance, but not faultless. He admitted they had been skilfully manipulated, involving the use of filters and premium photo-editing software. If not for Paige's sharp eye, it was likely no one would have been any the wiser. Reuben's stomach knotted when he and Lydia were discussing this on Skype, late one afternoon while Paige and he were in Atlanta. Paige, although within hearing range if they needed her input, was currently engrossed in replying to emails.

"How do we handle this then?" he asked. "Do we have any evidence as to who took the photographs?"

"I asked one of my colleagues in our LA office to do some digging. Seems the guy your Erin wants to marry, is quite the technical whiz, and was once a professional photographer. I have it on good authority, he possesses the talent required for such an enterprise. Shame he couldn't use it for less questionable ends. We're pretty sure it's him; Erin wouldn't want to risk involving an outsider." Lydia paused. "With your permission, I would like to see how far

Erin is prepared to push this angle. Hang on..." when Reuben started to interrupt, "...I won't allow anything to be published. Trust me, Reuben. She's already on very shaky legal ground, because this amounts to blackmail, but I think it could prove interesting, and to our benefit, if we let her think she's got us running scared."

Reuben pondered Lydia's suggestion. The whole thing left a bitter taste in his mouth, and he would prefer it to be finished as quickly as possible, but had to admit, playing Erin at her own game held a certain appeal.

"Fine, I'm angry enough to let her dig herself deeper. Do I have to do anything?"

"I shall reply to her attorney to let them know we have passed on the images and are awaiting your instructions. We think Erin might try to contact you directly. When she came to see you in San Francisco, she probably assumed your conversation gave her an opening, and now she'll try to pressure you in some way or other. I suggest you tape any discussions. This is a divorce case; such things are not unanticipated."

"Not sure how she'll manage that, she doesn't know my 'phone number. She *might* know my email, but it's unlikely, bearing in mind we didn't have such things thirty odd years ago. Anyway, if by chance she does, I'll forward anything on to you without responding. Oh, and by the way, she's not *my* Erin."

Reuben sighed and it seemed to come from his boots.

"You okay, Reuben?" Lydia asked in mild concern.

"Not really. This whole thing stinks."

"It does, but I did warn you. Divorce is an ugly business."

They discussed the matter for a few more minutes but it

was late evening in London, and shortly thereafter, said their goodbyes.

Reuben remained where he was sitting, mulling over the whole sorry scenario. Four months ago, he was happily unaware of what was about to happen. He was looking forward to Christmas and then this tour. One letter had thrown his world into a spin, and he was beginning to wonder whether it would ever stabilise again. The *only* positive to come out of it, was meeting Paige.

He glanced across the room. Paige was sitting cross-legged on one of the armchairs, typing rapidly on her laptop. Her expression was one of complete concentration, her nose crinkling occasionally while she worked. Bathed in the warm glow of one of the ceiling spotlights, her hair — which was falling around her shoulders — resembled molten toffee, and Reuben, as ever, itched to tangle his fingers through it.

What would they do when they got back to England? Their lives, their homes, were miles apart. Could they make it work? Here they were cocooned from their everyday world, and long-distance relationships were notoriously fraught. Reuben closed his eyes; to leave Rosedale Abbey was unthinkable, to lose Paige — unimaginable.

"What's up?" Paige's quiet voice broke through his introspection.

"I'm just think how lovely this has been, but that in a few days, we have to go back to reality and all that entails."

"What do you mean?"

"We live so far apart, how are we going to make this work?"

"I'm sure we'll find a way. Weekends, holidays..." She shrugged, reluctant to admit she didn't want to be apart from Reuben. The idea of saying goodbye at the end of every weekend made her chest pinch.

"I don't want this to be weekends and holidays, I'm beyond all that. I want you in my life not skirting the periphery of it."

"I want that too, but..."

"...but your job is in London, and mine is in Yorkshire. I know, I know. I should be the one to move. My research is not fixed to a place, but I cannot work in a city, I've tried it and it's hopeless. I need peace and quiet. I realise it sounds selfish, but I guess it's just the way I'm wired."

Paige put her laptop to one side, uncoiled her legs, and walked over to where Reuben was sitting on the edge of the bed. "Don't apologise for who and how you are, Reuben. I could no more drag you away from Moorview than swim the Channel. My one visit was enough to convince me of that. We'll work it out." She cupped his cheek, her thumb brushing the corner of his mouth. "We'll work it out," she repeated gently, and kissed him. "Now, I think it's time for a drink and then we need to decide where we're going to have dinner. Let's not worry about all the whys and wherefores until we get home. These things have a habit of sorting themselves out, once you stop trying to force an answer."

"I s'pose," Reuben agreed and gave a lopsided smile. Drawing Paige close for another kiss, he relished the way she responded, the way his own body responded. It was a gift, this chance — to love another so profoundly was like his heart's second sigh. For years, Reuben's heart had been protected behind an impenetrable shield, for to be rejected so unequivocally was almost unbearable. Then came Paige who, without trying, had chipped away at his self-imposed barriers and, although his heart was now exposed, this time he relished it.

. . .

For the first time in longer than he cared to count, Reuben wanted to take that risk.

The one he never dreamed he would take again.

17

To Reuben's relief, Erin didn't try to get in touch with him, or at least if she did, her attempts were blocked. That she was party to such an outrageous scheme continued to rankle, and Reuben acknowledged to himself, he probably never knew her at all. He thought about the day he received the letter from Erin's attorney's and Alex's reaction when he did not deny he still loved his wife. What an idiot. Holding a candle for someone all those years. What a bloody waste. Although perhaps, not a complete waste. If he had divorced Erin sooner — had he known her where-abouts — he probably would not have met Paige; so — silver linings and all that.

The following week, Reuben was back at Moorview.

The remainder of the tour went well and Joel, on behalf of the publishing house, had declared the whole exercise a resounding success. The evening prior to their departure, Joel, Paige, and Reuben enjoyed a celebratory meal and toasted their achievement, with more than a glass or two of champagne, after which goodbyes were said, and agreements were made to keep in touch.

The next morning Reuben and Paige flew to London.

———

Leaving Paige at Heathrow was one of the hardest things Reuben had ever done, but they each had commitments at opposite ends of the country, and Reuben had a connecting flight to catch.

"I'll call as soon as I get home. I hate saying goodbye like this, it sucks," Reuben said when they parted.

Paige's smile seemed a little strained, while she hugged him close. "I miss you already," she murmured against his cheek.

"Not as much as I miss you." He kissed her, then cupped her face and looked her in the eye for a long moment. "I love you, Paige Latimer, and I'll see you as soon as I can wangle it."

"I love you too, Reuben Faulkner, now go before I make a complete idiot of myself." She pushed him gently. Without looking back, Paige hurried towards the station to catch a train into the city, while Reuben followed the signs for the transfer bus to Terminal Five.

Another three hours of sitting around, either in the departure lounge or on the plane and he was home. Jake and Alex picked him up at Leeds-Bradford Airport, and the journey to Rosedale Abbey was surprisingly restful. The traffic wasn't too bad, and Reuben was content to watch the Yorkshire landscape whiz by, while his son and daughter-in-law chattered about this and that, their conversation wafting over him. He knew Paige was home; he received her text when he disembarked from his flight, replying that he'd call her later.

It had been a long day, but Reuben wanted to feel the soft North Yorkshire air on his skin, breathe it into his lungs. After a rapturous welcome by the melee of dogs, all of whom went bananas the instant he walked through the door — Reuben carried his suitcase through to his wing of the house. He stood for a long moment in the dearly familiar room, soaking it all in. He closed his eyes and thanked whichever god might have been responsible that Erin could *not* get her hands on this. Without bothering to unpack, he shrugged into a warm jacket, and headed for the kitchen.

"Want a cuppa?" Alex asked, when he entered.

"Not right now, Alex, thanks all the same. I think I'll take the dogs for a quick walk. I need to stretch my legs after so long sitting."

Alex grinned and nodded her understanding. "Totally get that. I can't wait to be out onto the moor the minute I get home, even if I've only been away a day! Have fun, yell when you come in and I'll have a whisky poured!"

"Sounds good, won't be long." Reuben gathered four of their five dogs — Bruno, Alex's aged wolfhound being far too old for even the shortest walk — clipped on their leashes and was soon striding up the rise onto the edge of the moor. So early in the year, the daylight was already waning, and the air was cold, but not uncomfortably so. Reuben walked steadily for fifteen minutes and, coming to a high point, stopped and turned around slowly, the view in every direction — spectacular.

He had missed this.

He was home.

.   .   .

He pulled his phone out of his pocket and, searching his contacts, hit the call icon for Paige. She answered instantly

"Reuben, you're home, how is everything, I miss you." Her words came out in a rush, making Reuben chuckle.

"Yes, I'm home, up on the moor to be exact, and it's almost perfect."

"Almost?" He could hear the puzzlement in her voice. "Why what's wrong?"

"You're not here to share it with me."

"Oh, Reuben you do say the most romantic things." She sighed audibly. "I wish I was there.

"Me too, hopefully soon. Does Lydia know you're back?"

"Yeah, I rang her a little while ago, but I'm not going to talk shop today. That can wait 'til tomorrow. Today, I'm still kind of on holiday. I'm planning a takeaway, a large glass of wine and some crappy television for the evening. You?"

"Thankfully, Alex and Jake are here, otherwise I'd probably be living on mouldy bread. I have a hunch there's a stew in the oven, complete with dumplings, if the heavenly aroma is anything to go by. Preceded by a large whisky."

They chatted for a while longer, then said goodbye, promising to talk again before they went to bed. The dogs were milling around, wanting to be on the move, and Reuben continued on the same path for another half an hour.

The rest of the day and evening was spent with the three discussing the recent developments in Reuben's divorce proceedings. He revealed Erin's latest ploy and showed them the pictures. Jake and Alex were appalled, especially once they knew the full extent, and that they had been unwitting participants in the scam.

"How could she do this to you, to Jake?" Alex queried, stunned.

"No idea. I am as staggered as you. All I can say is thank goodness for Paige. I knew I was innocent of what the pictures implied, but she was the one who spotted the flaws. Not sure what Lydia is waiting for, possibly some ridiculous demand, before she fires her own salvo. It would be interesting to be a fly on the wall of Erin's attorney's office when she does."

"Maybe she'll invite you down to their offices so you can sit in on the meeting. Oh, if she doesn't, why not suggest it? Do a video conference between offices with all of you involved. That way her reactions can be on camera!"

Reuben laughed at her eager face. "Alex Faulkner, should I be worried at how excited you are over hoisting someone with their own petard?" he asked, raising an amused brow at Jake.

"I think my wife's penchant for lurid detective stories has a lot to answer for." Jake grinned, and suffered a shove to the shoulder. "Ooof, no need for violence."

"Laugh away, I cannot think of a nicer way for karma to bite her on the bum," Alex replied pertly. "Nothing more than she deserves." She paused then added, "Did you tell her by the way?"

"Tell who what?" Jake stared at her in puzzlement.

"Not you. Reuben, did you tell Paige?"

Jake swung his gaze to his father. "Dad? What's she going on about?"

"Do you mean you didn't tell Jake? I am amazed."

"Not my story to share, I knew you'd tell him, eventually." Alex shrugged nonchalantly.

"Dad... what?"

Reuben put Jake out of his misery and rather diffidently elaborated. "Paige and I are seeing each other, or dating...

whatever it's called these days. It's still very new, but I think, I hope she will agree to it becoming something... errr... permanent in the not too distant future."

Jake gawped at his father. "Wait, you're telling me in the middle of divorcing Erin..." he could never quite bring himself to refer to her as his mother, "...you fall for another woman?"

18

Unaccustomed heat flooded Reuben's cheeks. Lordy, he felt like a schoolboy. "Yes, Jake, I did and don't make it sound like I planned this, because it came completely out of left field. Until recently, I thought Erin was my one and only. I haven't looked at another woman since she left, which was another reason why I was suspicious of those photos. I was quite happy with the status quo. Single life has treated me well and I reckon I didn't do too bad a job as a parent. Then I met Paige..." he hesitated, "now I can't imagine my life without her." This last came out in a rush.

"I, for one, am ecstatic," Alex beamed at her father-in-law and stood up, squeezing his shoulder as she walked past him. "I'm going to check the dinner," she said, tactfully leaving father and son alone.

Peace descended on the room, the only sound, the crackle of firewood in the hearth and the gentle snoring of five tired dogs.

. . .

"So, it's that serious?" Jake asked after a lengthy silence. "I'm not blind. I saw how you two behaved around each other at the Grand Canyon, but I never guessed how important Paige is to you. Still can't believe Alex didn't tell me."

"I asked her not to say anything until after we left, but totally expected her fill you in then. She's a good girl, and yes, it *is* serious. I'd marry Paige tomorrow if I could... but..." Reuben let that hang. "Jake, I know this might seem impulsive, but trust me. I am not rushing into this without due thought. I might be in my sixties but I'm not senile."

"Dad, I never thought you were, it's only..."

"What... you think after thirty odd years on my own, I'm not entitled to a little happiness?"

"That's not it at all. I just worry..."

"Son, Paige isn't Tricia or Jill. The circumstances under which we met are entirely different. You ought to be questioning her sanity not mine. Who'd want to take me on with all the crap floating about at the moment?"

"True enough," Jake conceded with a wicked grin. "You're not that much of a catch." His grin becoming outright laughter at Reuben's outraged expression. "You left yourself wide-open for that. Joking aside, Dad, I just don't want you hurt again."

"I get that, and I'm grateful, but you need to trust me, and Paige for that matter. We aren't naive kids. We've been there and done that. Will you be alright with me asking her to marry me? When I manage to pluck up the courage that is."

Jake studied his father, noting a simmering joy he didn't think he'd ever seen on Reuben's face. If Paige was the one who put it there, she was okay in his book. "If she makes you happy, that's all I need to know," he raised a hand, palm out, "and, by that, I do mean all. It's one thing knowing your father is in love, quite another to hear the sordid details."

"Deal... but they are not sord—"

"Dad... please... come on." Jake's expression was horrified.

Reuben sniggered. "Talk about leaving yourself wide open. That was too easy, Son, way too easy. Now let's go see what Alex is doing with dinner."

The subject was dropped, more or less, and the rest of the evening passed pleasantly with gossip about what Alex and Jake had been doing in his absence.

The conversation he had with Paige just before he turned in, was too short, but better than nothing.

Soon, all at Moorview were fast asleep.

The next morning, Reuben spoke with Lydia, who, before he could even broach Alex's suggestion, invited him to London to participate in a video chat with Erin's lawyers.

"I would like you to be there when we tell them what we have uncovered. There is a slim possibility they are unaware of how she came into possession of those images, but they saw fit to use them without verifying their accuracy, so tough."

"I'll be there, day and time?"

"Monday, five-thirty in the afternoon, that's nine thirty in the morning for them. Hang on, I have Paige here, she wants a quick word. See you on Monday."

Reuben heard a murmured conversation then,

"Hi Reuben."

"Hey, beautiful. How's tricks?"

"Pretty good now I'm talking to you." He knew she was smiling by her tone. "Any chance you can come down on Friday? Gives us a whole weekend. You can stay with me, if that's not too... err..."

"I'd love to, thanks for the offer. I'll see whether I can get a train which'll get me into Kings Cross about four-ish. I could meet you at your office if you like?"

"Sounds like a plan. Unless I can wangle an early finish. Gotta go, talk this evening?"

"Absolutely," he hesitated, adding quietly, "I love you."

"I love you too. See you Friday. Ohhh, can't wait."

"Me neither..." He grinned as she hung up.

Friday was only three days away, hopefully he could get a train. Not the best timing, but at least it wasn't school holidays. He opened his internet browser and checked for seats. There were several available in First Class, which made it a bit pricey, but he decided it was worth it, so booked it and also his return journey for the Tuesday afternoon. At least this way, if he had to change his ticket it should only cost the admin charge, which wasn't excessive. He pinged a text to Paige to let her know, then buckled down to work.

Hours later, after answering a seemingly endless number of emails and, after making sure any other housekeeping and administration, book-wise, was complete, Reuben was standing at the back door, breathing in the fresh spring air while sipping a hot coffee brewed in his favourite mug. It *was* good to be home. His thoughts, as ever, circling how he and Paige could make this work. Movement behind, made him glance over his shoulder. Alex was walking towards him.

"Okay?" she asked.

"Yep, just mulling over life the universe and everything."

"Paige?" she hazarded.

"Some…"

"Not much you can do until the divorce is settled. Any chance she could work from here, you know be like a satellite member of staff?"

"I guess that might be a possibility. I have to go to London this weekend, hopefully we can chat about options. Lydia has arranged a video conference for Monday afternoon with Erin's lawyers. Fingers crossed we can put an end to all this messing about and just agree terms."

"You aren't going to give her any money, are you?"

"Not if I can help it. I might have considered it, but she's blown any sympathy I might have been harbouring, with this stunt. Even though we know it's a set up, it still nauseates me. I wake up in a cold sweat." Reuben raked a hand through his hair. "How can something, which was once so wonderful become so tawdry?"

Alex shrugged. "You're asking the wrong person. I've experienced the tawdry, but it was never wonderful to start with, I have no clue. I *can* tell you how tawdry becomes wonderful though… which is kind of what's happening with you and Paige." She slipped her arm through Reuben's and hugged him. "'Nother coffee?" she asked, disappearing into the kitchen when he nodded.

Reuben turned away from the sunny afternoon and headed back inside.

Work awaited.

19

Late Friday afternoon saw Paige dancing about on the platform at King's Cross, waiting for Reuben's train. It had been delayed slightly at Peterborough, for which she was thankful because it gave her the extra few minutes, she wanted to make sure she looked presentable after a mad dash across London at peak hour.

The minute Paige saw Reuben alight, she darted around the other passengers, who were walking towards her in a wave, and all but leapt into his arms, which immediately tightened around her. Reuben bent his head to kiss her soundly, both of them ignoring the odd wolf-whistle.

"Hi," he said eventually, lifting his head to smile a greeting.

"Hi, yourself." Paige grinned, happily.

Taking her hand, he entwined their fingers. They strolled along the concourse to the tube station and, in a little under an hour, were walking up the quiet street where Paige lived.

"This is me," she said a trifle self-consciously, flinging her free hand towards a tall, narrow house tucked in the middle of the lengthy terrace.

"It's lovely, Paige." Reuben smiled as they entered her home. Three storeys high, the coloured brickwork, steep roof, and fancy trim around the gable, indicated it was probably built in the Victorian era. The interior was tastefully decorated. Mostly pastels balanced by an occasional, richly patterned rug or bright curtains. "This is a great spot to live. Quiet, yet a pretty quick commute."

"I know, I do love it. I grew up here, this was my parents' house. I'm an only child and when they died, they left me everything. Dad was pretty savvy; they owned this outright. I have no mortgage and was able to afford the necessary renovations, re-wiring and so forth. I all but gutted the place, it was desperate. I did keep any original features where possible, like the fireplaces and the tiled floors. I even managed to get double glazing without damaging those of the windows which have stained-glass. Cost me a bit, but definitely worth it."

"You've done an amazing job, you thought about doing this for a living?" Reuben teased gently.

"Hahaha... funny guy. I used to want to, but people can be soooo picky. I don't think I'd have the patience to listen to them harping on about a bespoke marble bench top made by pixies, because so and so got one and it was *just awesome.*" Paige mimicked the participants on television shows who did precisely that, batting her eyelashes and pouting.

Reuben guffawed. "Okay, maybe not... but you do have a talent for it."

"Less talk about decorating and more kissing," Paige admonished gently. "I'm sure you'll want to... err... unpack... the bedroom's this way," she continued and, slipping out of his arms, led the way upstairs.

The weekend went by far too quickly, but they relished the

intimacy of being together with no call on their time. It was like a mini holiday; sleeping in, followed by unhurried days, topped off with lazy evenings watching movies after a meal out. Paige's home was close to Hampstead Heath, and the couple enjoyed several extended walks around it. The weather was mild and sunny; the ground carpeted in spring flowers and the trees cloaked in greens of every hue. They talked, and laughed, discovering even more about the other. It was one of those weekends they would remember for a long time.

Monday came around too quickly, and Paige had to be at work at 8:30. Reuben said he wanted to be a tourist for a day, intent on going to the Tower.

By 5p.m., he was in Lydia's office, preparing for the meeting. He admitted to feeling a trifle nervous, but was more interested in the opposing attorneys' reaction to what Lydia was about to reveal. Cup of strong coffee in hand, all he could do now, was wait.

5:30p.m., on the dot, the connection blinked into life. Reuben found himself staring at two men and one woman — all dressed in power suits and all dripping wealth. *Good to see where all their fees go,* he thought, cynically.

"Good afternoon, Lydia," one of them said, his West Coast accent sounding odd in a room full of British lawyers.

Lydia greeted all three and made the introductions. "Where's Mrs Faulkner?" she queried, the latter conspicuous by her absence.

"Unfortunately, we have no idea," the woman, Miranda Butler, replied. "We received emailed confirmation she would be here, but so far she's a no show."

"You requested this meeting and I am not prepared to

discuss final settlement without her in attendance, is this another delaying tactic?" Lydia's voice was chill.

"Honestly, we expected her to be here."

Lydia pressed the mute button and looked at the other people in the room with her — Paige, Reuben and two article clerks. "What do you reckon? Start the ball rolling and see where it takes us?" There were four nods of consent.

Reuben glanced at his watch. This was typical of Erin; she was still making everyone dance to her tune. He tried to concentrate on proceedings, inwardly seething.

Meanwhile two hundred miles away at the edge of a sleepy village nestled in the Yorkshire moors, Alex was disturbed by a loud rapping on the front door. She glanced at her watch, almost half five, it was late for someone to be calling. Saving her work, Alex frowned, wondering who it could be.

You expecting anyone, Jake?" she called to her husband who was working in his own office adjacent to the kitchen.

"Nope, maybe it's someone trying to sell us something," came his amused reply.

"Damned inconsiderate to be calling this late," Alex grumbled. She opened the door, a welcoming smile on her face, which fell when she recognised the person at the other side. Schooling her features, Alex strove for calm. "May I help you?" she enquired, politely.

"I'm looking for a Professor Faulkner, who used to live here. I assume he still does, since it mentions in his bio that his home is in the Yorkshire moors."

Alex, whose stare was nothing short of glacial, contemplated the visitor; the audacity of the woman confounded her. "He's not here. I'm sorry, but your journey was wasted," she replied. Her tone was bland, but she was struggling to remain calm. What Alex *really* wanted to do, was punch the woman's lights out... perhaps not the most dignified response.

"Oh, what a shame. I hoped I might be able to persuade him to talk with me, privately. He hasn't answered any of my emails, so I took a chance." Erin Faulkner offered what Alex supposed was a winsome smile.

"Unfortunately, that's impossible. I'm uncertain when he's due back." Alex, fighting her temper, willed herself not to slap this woman who had caused so much anguish.

"And you are...?" Erin quizzed.

"Who I am is not really any of your business, is it?" Alex replied, loftily.

"Oh, you must be his latest fling. You do know he can never stick with one woman, or man for that matter, for more than a couple of months." With a bored sigh, Erin glanced down at her hand, studying her fingernails — manicured to perfection and painted dark purple.

Alex wasn't fooled, and felt her jaw drop at the woman's insinuation, at the same time as she heard Jake's footsteps on the stone floor. He came up behind her and placed the palm of his hand gently against her back. He filled the door-way, his height making Erin take a step back.

"Please do not tell me you just said that?" Jake interposed. He sounded relaxed, but Alex could feel the tension radiating from his taut frame, and knew his anger was smouldering.

"Goodness, a ménage," she trilled with a sly smile. "How very open-minded he's become. I'm Erin Faulkner by the way, Reuben's wife." She paused for effect, her brow creasing when neither Alex nor Jake reacted.

"Oh, right. Wait... aren't you supposed to be at a conference call today regarding your settlement?" Jake enquired, after several seconds when no one spoke, for all the world as though he had just recalled the identity of their visitor — still giving nothing away.

"Oh that, my lawyers can deal with it. I daresay Reuben will give me what I've asked for."

"Why should he?" Jake's apparently innocuous question caused Erin's flawless features to darken.

"Because he owes me. I wasted four and a half years of my life waiting for him to *be* someone. Now he is, and I only want what's mine by rights," she blustered, common sense deserting her.

Jake saw no reason to explain who he was or what he knew. He stood there and appraised the woman who gave birth to him. For so long he had wondered how he would feel, should they ever meet again. He had no recollection of her, at all, and looking at her petulant face, was oddly glad.

"Well, when is Reuben expected back?" Erin demanded.

"No idea," Jake grinned wolfishly. "He's a grown man, he doesn't need to tell us what he's up to. Might I suggest you scuttle back to whichever hole you crawled out of and don't bother us again."

"My, aren't you the charmer? What *does* Reuben see in you? You must be good in the sack, that's all I can say."

20

The sound of Jake inhaling sharply, prompted Alex to press her hand on his arm, knowing this was about to escalate. He turned his head and smiled down at his wife.

"I've got this," he murmured and, leaning down, kissed the top of her head. He took Alex's hand, feeling her squeeze his lightly when their fingers met.

When Jake spoke, his voice vibrated with scarcely suppressed fury. "Mrs Faulkner, it may come as a shock to learn, you have just accused your son and his wife, of having sex with his father. It might also surprise you to know, your attempt to blackmail your husband has backfired dismally. Now, if that's all, please leave my property. How you have the temerity to come here is beyond me. You are not welcome. Any sympathy you assume you are due was erased the minute you abandoned us. Furthermore, you might have given birth to me, but you are not, and never have been, my mother." Jake's lip curled in distaste, and he moved to slam the door.

"Wait... please." Erin's plea rang out. There was something in her voice and, against his better judgement, Jake hesitated. "You're Jake?"

He inclined his head.

"Holy *crap*!" She expelled a breath. "Shit, I'm sorry." She pressed her hands to burning cheeks and shook her head. "God, it's been thirty-four years. Jake..." Her voice trailed off.

"So what? What do you care? You turn up here out of the blue and, without so much as a by your leave, insult my wife, my father, and me. If you want to talk to Dad, he's in London, about to speak to your attorneys who, I imagine, expected you to be in their offices in San Francisco. What the hell are you thinking, *Mrs Faulkner*?" Unable to help himself, Jake sneered the last two words.

An uncomfortable silence fell. The three studied each other for what seemed an age, then Erin's shoulders sagged, and she seemed to diminish in stature, as though deflating.

Seeing Jake, her son, her only child — tall, handsome and apparently happily married — somehow gave Erin a jolt of reality. Made her see her actions for what they were. Vulgar, cheap, and sordid. *God, she was a first-class bitch. What happened to her... she never used to be so awful... did she?* Then she recalled exactly how awful she had been. She had abandoned her child, removed herself from his life, vanishing with no explanation. *Who does that? Was there any chance she could make amends?*

"I don't know. I spoke with your father when he was in San Francisco, did he tell you?" She glanced warily at Jake.

"He mentioned he'd seen you, but that was all."

"I asked him whether we could get together to talk, and

he declined. I got angry and... well... I think it got out of hand."

"You're not kidding. *Out of hand...* that's the bloody understatement of the year," Alex snapped.

Jake bit down on a bark of laughter. Abruptly, the whole situation struck him as completely bizarre. "Hang on, this is ridiculous." He withdrew his phone from his pocket and rang Reuben's number.

"Jake? What's wrong?" His father's anxious tones floated out of the speaker.

"Dad, I have someone here who needs to talk to you." Jake handed the phone to Erin. "Don't walk away from the front door, the signal isn't that strong once you are a few feet from the house. Fix it," he instructed. Slipping an arm around Alex, he ushered her back inside, leaving a dazed Erin stammering a 'hello' into the phone.

In London, Reuben was looking at his phone in shock. *Erin was at Moorview, what the actual...?* He put it on speaker and laid it on the desk between them, so everyone in the office could hear.

"Erin? What are you doing in Yorkshire? You're supposed to be elsewhere."

"I wanted to talk to you, to see whether..."

"Whether I could be blackmailed?" Reuben interjected.

"No, not really, well... not blackmail as such..."

"Erin, we know the images were doctored. We have just informed your lawyers, who have every right to sever all ties with you, as well as take any action against you and whatsis-name — Dean is it? — they see fit." Reuben paused to let his words sink in. "Erin, I don't think you understand what you did to Jake and me all those years ago. Why didn't you simply ask for a divorce? Yes, it would have hurt, but we could have dealt with it like adults. But oh, no, you decided to do a runner, and vanished without trace. Not a single call, or letter in thirty odd years, then you think it's okay to demand more than half of my assets. Get real. Even then, I *might* have been persuaded to give you a decent settlement, had you not resorted to creating those images and threatening to destroy my life. Your son was in one of those photos, did you know that?"

He could hear the anger in his voice and strove for calm.

"Erin, I wish you all the best with your life, truly I do and, because of what we once shared, I will agree not to press charges against you and Dean for what the pair of you tried to do. This is on the proviso, you withdraw your claim for monetary recompense for the four years we were married. What your attorneys do is their call. There will be no money, no division of assets. You go your way, I'll go mine. The settlement will be on the grounds of being apart for longer than the requisite period."

There was a protracted silence then he heard a resigned sigh. "Fine, I agree. Reuben..." She stopped speaking.

"What?" His tone was hard... flat.

"I realise an apology isn't even close to enough, but I *am* sorry. I've been a bitch. I can't offer any real reason for why I left. I was young and thoughtless and, absurd as it sounds, didn't think you or Jake would miss me. Once I was back home, it was easier to pretend you didn't exist than deal with the guilt and, until I met Dean, had no desire for that kind of commitment again. Yes, I agree with whatever you decide, and thank you for not pressing charges." She drew a shuddering breath. "Maybe one day you'll be able to forgive me. I'll hang up now and call my lawyers immediately. Hopefully, we can sort this out quickly."

Before she could hang up, Reuben spoke once again. "Erin,"

"Yes."

"Thank you. I know that must have been hard. One last thing. Our son is an amazing man. He is a successful engineer with his own consultancy, who has been married to Alex a little over two years. He is well-grounded, sensible, respectful, and has a big heart. Despite everything, you are responsible for some of that." He smiled gently and glanced across at Paige who smiled back.

Erin's voice wavered a little. "Th-thank you, Reuben, that's very kind, certainly much kinder than I'd probably be if the circumstances were reversed. I appreciate it." They heard her inhale another deep breath. "Okay, I'm going. No doubt, you'll hear from my lawyers shortly when they've stopped reaming me out. Bye." The call was cut off before anyone would reply.

Reuben looked at the other four in the room. "Wow, that was *not* what I anticipated, when I arrived here an hour ago."

"I think it's done, bar the shouting." Lydia nodded at the two article clerks. "Draw up the paperwork so I can check it and send it over before I finish today." They scuttled out, leaving Lydia, Paige, and Reuben.

"Okay, the day's over, you two should get out of here. Reuben, please don't leave London until we've got this signed, which will probably not be until tomorrow or the day after given the time difference." Lydia gathered her sheaf of documents and, without waiting for his reply, left the room.

Reuben remained where he was sitting, absorbing his conversation with Erin. "Do you suppose if I'd agreed to meet her when we were in the States, I could have avoided this debacle?" he asked Paige.

"No, I think that would have simply muddied the waters. I think, until about half an hour or so ago, Erin was hellbent on screwing you out of everything. Something Jake said to her has caused this unexpected about face. You're right, your son is an amazing man." Paige smiled and stood to walk around to where Reuben was sitting. "Home?"

"Absolutely!"

21

In Rosedale Abbey, Erin, using her own mobile phone, had spoken at length with her attorneys. It was rather an acrimonious conversation and she was trembling by the time the call ended. Rapping quietly on the front door, she handed Jake his phone when he appeared. Thanking him, Erin was about to leave, when his next words halted her.

"Would you like a cuppa before you set off back?"

She gawked at him in disbelief. "I b-beg your p-pardon," she stuttered.

"Come on, you look like you could use a good strong coffee. Where are you staying tonight?"

"Y-York..." she managed. Then, after swallowing twice in an attempt to clear a suddenly clogged throat, continued, "... really? You would invite me into your home after everything I've done?"

"Nothing to do with me. This was Alex's idea, but she's right, a puff of wind would blow you over right now, and it would be irresponsible to let you drive in that state." Jake softened his words with a slight smile — so like Reuben's, Erin blinked.

"Thank you, if you are absolutely sure."

"I am absolutely sure." He stood aside, allowing her to enter the home she left more than three decades previously.

By the time Erin drove out of the little village, the fragments of a relationship, presumed permanently shattered, were slowly being repaired. It would not be easy, and would doubtless take a long, *long* time — for Jake, especially, the anger ran deep — but at least there was a glimmer of hope.

The following day, Erin took the train to London, seeking the firm of Tomlinson, Draper, and Vaughan, which she discovered to be discreetly housed in an unassuming Georgian-era building on the corner of a leafy square. She was shown into Lydia's office, whereupon the latter closed the door and, after sending a brief message to Paige, engaged Erin in a serious and protracted discussion.

An hour later, Reuben arrived. He had not expected to see his almost ex-wife, but it gave the proceedings a sense of completion. Their conversation was cordial, bordering on amicable and, when Lydia spoke to Erin's attorneys at the end of the afternoon, she affirmed the relevant documents had been submitted to the courts and the fees paid.

Now, it was just a matter of time. Erin and Reuben were married in England; thus, its dissolution would be dealt with under the British judicial system.

Erin advised them her return flight to the States was booked for the coming Friday, and thus, would be available for the remainder of the week, if needed. Reuben also delayed his return to Moorview until Friday, Paige agreeing to travel north with him for the weekend.

Finally, five months after Reuben received the first communique from Erin's attorneys, he could see a light at the end of a very dark tunnel. He and Erin had reached a tentative accord, Jake was cautiously rebuilding a connection with his mother, and he, Reuben had found the love of his life. Granted, this last had happened rather later than usual, but that didn't mean it was any less profound, or treasured.

Friday afternoon, Reuben and Paige alighted from the train at Thirsk, to be met by Jake and Alex, who treated them to a bar snack at one of their favourite pubs. Paige had an attack of nerves when they drove up to Moorview — this was the first time she would be spending the night in Reuben's home. She wasn't given much chance to feel awkward, however, welcomed, boisterously, by the four of the five dogs; Bruno thumped his tail, enthusiastically but did not deign to vacate his comfortable bed.

"See, you're already one of the family." Alex grinned when Paige was allowed to stand again, the dogs turning their attention to Reuben.

"Thank you for having me here," Paige said, shyly. "I know it can't be easy, especially after..."

"Paige, you make Dad happier than I've ever seen him, please don't apologise for that." Jake countered with a grin. "Mind, hurt him and you'll regret it." He winked, taking the threat from his remark.

"Jake!" Reuben expostulated, "Really! Do you *have* to be quite so dramatic? I am capable of looking after myself, you know. Sorry, Paige."

"It's okay, Reuben," Paige placated. "I get it. Trust me, Jake, I have absolutely no intention of hurting your father..." she paused, and her cheeks bloomed a delightful pink, "... ever." Reuben reached over and took her hand, bringing her knuckles to his lips. "Who could ever tire of such chivalry?" She smiled and closed the gap between them, sliding her free hand around his waist.

"Anyone for tea? Coffee?" Alex poked her head out of the kitchen.

"I'd love a tea," Paige replied, stepping back from Reuben.

"On it. Once you've got sorted, it'll be in the lounge."

Reuben, taking the hint, ushered Paige along the hall to his wing of the cottage. He switched on the light to reveal a surprisingly extensive and airy room, really more like a suite. The decor was understated but tasteful. The slightly uneven walls were painted in — what Paige later discovered was described as lace — a pastel pearly-cream hue. The thick pile wheat-coloured carpet all but demanded a person wriggle their toes through it. At the far side, facing a set of French doors, stood a comfortable-looking sofa in an interesting shade resembling antique bronze. The rich material was offset by two turquoise and cream patterned cushions, one in each corner of the chair — the trio of colours repeated in the curtains, which were currently closed. To Paige's left, a door led to what appeared to be a reasonably sized ensuite and, from where she was standing, she glimpsed same delicate shades in the tiles and vanity unit. The cleverly considered palate gave the room a tranquil ambience.

"This is beautiful," Paige breathed after several moments of silence while she surveyed the space.

"It's nice isn't it?" Reuben agreed, with one of his famous understatements. "Alex spent some time freshening up the place just after she and Jake were married. Until then, except for the guest rooms and the kitchen, everything was as it had been when I moved in." He shrugged, diffidently. "It was definitely due a revamp." He opened another door revealing a walk-in wardrobe. "There's space for you to hang your stuff, and that set of drawers is empty..." his smile was hesitant, doubtful almost.

"You sure you're okay with me sleeping in your room?" Paige eyed him speculatively. "I know this is a big deal for you."

"Hell, yes," came his emphatic reply.

"So, what's with this sudden reserve?"

Reuben folded his arms and leaned on the jamb of the bathroom door. "It's this." He waved his hand between Paige and her bags. "I hate this. I don't want to us to have a suit-case relationship. I know we've just spent over a week together, longer than we expected, but in two days' time, you'll be back on that damn train. Clearing space in my wardrobe, in my life seems... I don't know..." he opened his palms, struggling to articulate what he was trying to say, without totally freaking Paige out. "Sorry, ignore me... forget it. Let's go grab the cuppa Alex promised."

Paige watched Reuben rake his hand through his hair. His expression told her he would not discuss this further — at least, not tonight. "Just give me a few minutes to get changed and dig out my slippers," she said, "I'm sick of being in these heels. I can unpack properly later." She squeezed his hand. "Don't fret the small stuff, hon, we'll work it out."

Reuben searched her eyes, her exquisite sea-green eyes, for any sign she was pissed at him, to be met with nothing more than tender concern. "I love you, Paige Latimer," he murmured and gathered her close. He kissed her deeply and leisurely. Heady desire swirled around them, but Reuben deliberately held it at bay. They broke apart gasping. "Later," he promised.

"I'll hold you to that." She smiled against his mouth and,

briefly, rested her head on his shoulder, enjoying the strength of his arms encircling her.

In those few moments, Reuben made his decision. He acknowledged that to some it might seem precipitous, but Reuben had been waiting his whole life for Paige to walk into it and he wasn't going to waste another moment.

22

The next morning dawned bright, sunny, and the forecast was for a reasonably warm day — for the time of year. Reuben asked Paige whether she was up for a bit of a hike and a picnic. He suggested they take the dogs, set off over the moors, and see where the day took them.

"Sounds great, I'd love to, but I've only brought trainers with me. Will they be suitable? I don't own a pair of hiking boots."

"What's your shoe size?"

"I'm a six.

"Alex might have a pair that'll fit you, hang on."

Alex did, and an hour later — food and plenty of water safely stowed away in Reuben's backpack, with four dogs securely leashed up — they set out. Reuben led Paige through the gate at the rear of the garden and, skirting the neighbouring houses, followed the path into the village.

Reuben explained they would follow a sort of loose oval, going as far as the hamlet of Lastingham, returning via Chimney Bank, the steep hill leading into and out of one end of Rosedale Abbey. It was not too far, and he assured Paige the views were worth the walk. They joined the well-trodden bridleway, just outside the village, climbing steadily up the side of the moor.

The couple chatted while they walked. Reuben gave Paige a potted history of Rosedale Abbey and surrounding countryside. From first occupation at least ten thousand years ago during the Stone Age, through its many and varied chapters, reaching its heyday in the Victorian era when iron ore was discovered, to its tranquil existence nowadays — maintained despite its popularity with tourists. They stopped frequently so Paige could take a photo, or simply as an excuse for a kiss. The undulating vistas, and the ever-changing colours under a boundless azure sky were breathtaking.

"I know the Grand Canyon was impressive but, to me, this is much more spectacular," Paige said, just before they turned left towards Lastingham. "I can't explain why, it just is."

"I know what you mean," Reuben agreed. "The Grand Canyon has been there as long as, if not longer, than this landscape, but there is timeless allure about this area. It sneaks in under your defences and holds you captive. Once you fall in love, it will never let you go."

"Bit like you really." Turning until her butt was perched on the dry-stone wall they were standing beside, Paige grinned at Reuben, who flushed.

"Errr... I wasn't fishing."

She chuckled, "I know, that's what makes you so darn irresistible. The most romantic words fall from your lips, but you don't even register their double meaning. Anyone would think you were a writer."

"Irresistible, hey? I like that."

"Don't get cocky." She tapped him on the chest. "Now, did you say something about a pint?"

He dropped a kiss on her nose. "Let's do St Mary's first. It's lovely, has a crypt and everything." As they headed towards the churchyard, Reuben explained a monastery had been founded on the site in the mid-seventh century. The present church dated to the latter part of the eleventh century and had been a place of pilgrimage since at least that period. The crypt — deemed by those who make these decisions to be architecturally unparalleled — was also, arguably, the oldest Norman crypt in the world. Reaching the door, Reuben secured the dogs' leashes to an adjacent wooden bench, instructing them to 'stay'. Then he led Paige into the peace of the ancient church, where they spent a little while, lost in ecclesiastical history.

Whatever its claim to fame, Paige found the dim coolness of the hushed interior, soothing.

They came out into the bright daylight, to be met by four very excited dogs and, within moments, were sitting outside the Blacksmith's Arms, enjoying a welcome half-pint. Beer for Reuben, cider for Paige. They fell into the comfortable chitchat so familiar to them now, enjoying the warmth of the sun.

It would have been easy to while away the afternoon; basking in the almost summery weather, and watching the world go by — it's drowsy pace in keeping with the quiet of the village. So early in the year, and even though it was the weekend, tourists were few and far between. A couple of other walkers marched purposefully past, and one or two cyclists whizzed through. Other than that, it was just the locals going about their business.

"Come, on," Reuben said. He stood and, taking Paige's

hand, hauled her up. "If we stay here any longer, I'll be asleep."

"I know the feeling. I really shouldn't drink in the middle of the day, especially on an empty stomach." Paige chuckled, and wobbled dramatically to prove her point. "See..."

"Lightweight," Reuben grinned and drew her close to kiss her soundly.

"Not sure how that is supposed to help me stand up straight," she rasped when he lifted his head.

Unrepentant, Reuben grinned. "Just give it your best shot, if anyone asks, I'll tell them you're tipsy."

"Hey, that's unfair..."

With the dogs bounding alongside — stretching leashes to their fullest extent, thrilled at being on an adventure — the couple bantered back and forth, while they meandered out of the village. Not hurrying, they had all day. There was nothing to rush home for, and they still needed to find a dog-friendly picnic spot. Back on the moor, they ambled along the bridleway, once again stopping here and there to admire the view; the horizon in the far distance, hazy in the spring sunshine.

It didn't take them long to reach Ana Cross, a wayside monument indicating they were on the medieval route from Lastingham to the site of Rosedale Priory. Paige, not well-versed in medieval history, studied the waymarker for some time, asking questions about the priory and why a marker was required in the first place, which Rueben was able to answer in detail. She was astonished when he remarked, although it looked aged, this particular cross only dated back to about 1949, when the original was moved to the crypt of Lastingham church.

Marvelling at the 360-degree panorama, Paige asked whether having their lunch under the marker would be deemed disrespectful.

"I don't suppose so, and it's as good a place as any," was Reuben's considered response. He shrugged off the backpack and dug out the carefully wrapped sandwiches, packets of crisps, and bottles of water. Making themselves comfortable on the plinth, backs resting against the cool stone of the cross, the couple ate their picnic. There was no one else to be seen; the only sound was the snuffling of the dogs and the occasional cry of a moorland bird.

Picnic finished, Paige, replete and content, closed her eyes, breathed in the soft air, and tilted her face towards the sun. She could get used to this.

Reuben shot a glance at the woman who had captured his heart. It was only one day into her first weekend at Moorview yet, so seamlessly did she fit in, it was as though she had always been part of his home, his world. Paige belonged here. Unobtrusively, he slid his hand into the front pocket of the backpack, his fingers curling around the small object he'd secreted there while Paige was trying on Alex's walking boots. He smiled and withdrew his hand. Shuffling closer to Paige, he slung an arm around her. She twisted slightly, in order to rest her head on his shoulders. They stayed that way for a little while, relishing the togetherness; no cares, no need for conversation, just being at one with each other.

The breeze picked up, prompting Reuben to suggest they

get moving again. Paige agreed, albeit reluctantly. They checked to make sure any litter was collected, and tucked securely into the backpack, before setting off on the last, shortish leg of their walk. When they reached the top of Chimney Bank, at the bottom of which nestled Rosedale Abbey, Reuben paused and in the guise of reaching for his bottle of water, retrieved what he had hidden in the pocket. Replacing the bottle, he turned Paige — who was trying to spot Moorview — to face him.

"I know this might seem an odd place to say what I'm about to say, but I can't think of anywhere better, here with my favourite person in the world, overlooking my favourite place in the world." He smiled when Paige blushed. "Well it's true. Paige, you came into my life at a time when I was confused, hurt and angry. Everything I thought I knew was so screwed up, I could barely see straight. That you were even vaguely interested in me at all, never mind when I was at my lowest ebb, continues to amaze me. I know we haven't known each other very long, but I cannot imagine my life without you. So, before you come to your senses and skedaddle, please will you marry me?"

He opened the little box to reveal a ring of simple but effortlessly elegant design. A smooth curve of white gold cradled a glittering aquamarine flanked by two diamonds; the central gemstone almost exactly matching the colour of Paige's eyes.

Reuben held her gaze, watching those beautiful eyes widen in shock. "I know I'm not much of a catch. Hell, I'm not even divorced yet..." he grimaced self-consciously, "...but I love you more than life. It is as though you are my heart's second sigh. The one person who was able to steal in under my defences and make me feel whole again, the one person who feels like the other half of me. Dammit, I know I'm not explain—"

He didn't get chance to finish his sentence.

"YES!" Paige shouted her acceptance, flinging her arms around him and planting a searing kiss on his mouth. Yes! *Yes! Yes!*" she repeated, holding out her left hand for Reuben to slide the gleaming band over her third finger. Wonder of wonders, it fit! Paige was unaware Reuben had borrowed her one other ring as a guide... she hadn't even noticed it's day-long absence!

Waving her hand in the air, Paige executed a wild, happydance on the side of the road. "Reuben... I thought you'd never ask." She stopped jigging about and stepped back into his embrace.

Their lips met in sweet communion.

Their kiss — a promise, an affirmation... a forever.

23

EIGHT MONTHS LATER

It was nearly Christmas. The year seemed to have flown by. Looking back, Reuben found it hard to believe how much had happened. This time twelve months ago, he had just received the news Erin wanted a divorce. The woman who had walked out without a backward glance, the woman he had all but forgotten about, reappeared without warning, intent on flipping his life upside down — again. That her demand would lead to such unadulterated happiness still astounded him.

The ink was barely dry on his decree absolute when Reuben married Paige. They had a quiet, intimate ceremony at Duncombe Park in Helmsley, and then enjoyed a week's holiday — a wedding gift from Alex and Jake. That was four months ago, and the couple had settled quickly into married life. Their living arrangements presented the biggest hurdle, but eventually a compromise was reached.

Neither Paige nor Reuben could countenance spending the majority of the lives apart, and Paige was all set to resign from Tomlinson, Draper, and Vaughan, hoping to find a job closer to Rosedale Abbey. Lydia, however, did not want to lose her friend and employee — Paige had been with the law firm for over fifteen years and knew the company like the back of her hand. These days, that depth of knowledge was hard to come by.

Richard Tomlinson, possibly with the teeniest nudge from Alex, suggested Paige set up a satellite office in Thirsk. His law firm acted on behalf of the Lanchester estate in Northumberland, as well as several companies around Durham and York — thus, having a local representative would be beneficial. Coincidentally, Jake's engineering consultancy was based in Thirsk, and Paige had been fortunate enough to rent a suitable office space in the same building. The move was a great success, and Paige, who had been working there since about a month before the wedding, was slowly acclimatising to the less frantic pace. She decided to keep her home in London, which, currently, was rented out to one of her colleagues from head office.

Of Erin, Reuben had heard little, for which he was thankful. He no longer wished her ill but had no desire to further their relationship. She was part of his past and it was to there he relegated her. He knew she and Jake corresponded sporadically, but that was their business.

Today, a Tuesday, he was treating Paige to Christmas Tea at Castle Howard. The stately home — a favourite haunt of Reuben's, and somewhere he knew Paige wanted to visit — was usually decorated to a seasonal theme from mid-November, which was an added incentive behind his choice of destination.

It was a year since he met Paige and he was determined

to mark the occasion with something a little out of the ordinary. His wife had no idea where they were going, or the reason behind this trip in the middle of the week. All he had said was, to dress casually and wear comfortable shoes.

Castle Howard was just over half an hour's drive from Rosedale Abbey and the wintery landscape was breathtaking. The air was chill, hoar frost coated the trees and hedgerows, and a gossamer veil of mist hung over the fields.

"What a stunning day," Paige ventured while they motored along. "Glad you suggested I bring my thick coat."

"You won't need it for some of the day, but if we spend any time outdoors, you'll definitely want it." Reuben reached across and squeezed her jean-clad knee.

"I'm so excited. Pleeeeeease tell me where we're going," she beseeched, pouting when he shook his head.

"Nope, you have to wait and see," was all he would say. Reuben found Paige's enthusiasm for the simplest of things, endlessly gratifying. She didn't need to spend a fortune to have fun. A walk on the moor, or a picnic at the beach was as enjoyable to his wife as a holiday in Paris. So different from... he stopped that train of thought right there.

Shortly thereafter, they drew up in the car park. By now Paige knew where they were going and was all but jumping in her seat with excitement.

"I've *always* wanted to see Castle Howard," she gushed, "ever since I binge-watched Brideshead Revisited."

Reuben chuckled, "Come on then, grab your coat, make sure you have your gloves too." He opened Paige's door, helping her shrug into her warm jacket, before putting on his own coat.

. . .

It was a memorable day. They roamed the immaculately manicured grounds and spent hours exploring the house itself. During the afternoon, Reuben, finding a secluded corner, explained the reason why he wanted to do this today, rather than wait until the weekend.

"It's a year to the date, since you came to Moorview with Lydia. Even then, not knowing you from a bar of soap, I felt something. I didn't know what it was, but it shook me to my core. Anyway," he smiled rather shyly, "I just felt it merited acknowledging in more noteworthy style than cracking a bottle of champagne."

"Champagne would have been wonderful, but this, Reuben, this is extraordinary. Thank you." She leaned up to kiss him, the thrill he was hers forever, as always, stirring in her centre. She knew their coming together as a — for want of a better phrase — more mature couple, could have been problematic. Oddly, although both freely admitted they were set in their ways — used to doing things in a particular manner — and despite taking a little while to adjust to their idiosyncrasies, Paige and Reuben also discovered they complemented each other. It wasn't all wine and roses, they did have the occasional argument — which usually ended abruptly when Reuben kissed his wife into silence. It might not be the best method of resolving their differences, but it was by far the most fun.

"My pleasure, love." Reuben glanced at his watch. "Now where to next? We've got about half an hour before we need to be at the tearoom."

They decided to wander the grounds again and do the shops after high tea, which was everything they expected and more. Paige murmured that she felt like royalty, the staff was so attentive.

Stomachs full, they took their time pottering around the

shops, indulging in a mini-spending spree, using the fact Christmas was looming as an excuse.

They stayed until late afternoon. It was dusk when they eventually dragged themselves away, the clear sky auguring a frigid night ahead. Reuben drove home carefully, stopping on the way for a bar snack.

The couple returned to Rosedale Abbey mid-evening, the tires crunching on the gravel as they drove up to Moorview. Paige got out of the car and, although a little sleepy, was supremely happy. She stretched and paused for a moment to admire the sprawling cottage, whose lights spilled a welcoming glow onto the frosty garden; the scene recalling childhood fairy tales. Who would have thought, on this day, a year ago, she had just met the love of her life? Yes, perhaps somewhat belatedly and, although at the time, Paige would have rejected the notion it was love at first sight — looking back, she knew it had been. Their courtship — if one called it that these days... well they hadn't dated as such — was conducted in unorthodox circumstances, yet she believed that was what made them strong as a couple. They had endured *because* of the odds stacked against them, not in spite of them.

"You coming in, love, or are you going to stand there all night and freeze?" Reuben's amused question floated to her from the front door, already opened.

"Hmmmm...?" Paige's distracted reply, prompted him to walk over to where she was standing, lost in contemplation. He took her hand and drew her against him.

"Paige, sweetheart, it's icy out here. Come on inside where it's warm. There's a whisky in it," he cajoled.

His wife turned to him. He stole a quick kiss, and then paused, staring into her glorious eyes, those eyes which had held him captive from the first moment his gaze landed on them.

He felt his heart lift, swell and settle. "I love you, Paige Faulkner.

I love you, Reuben Faulkner. Now, what were you saying about a whisky?"

He chuckled and led her inside.

The door closed, and before long all was quiet.

———————

Life... love... is unpredictable, and often happens when least anticipated. The only decision is whether to reach out and grab it, or let it pass by, afraid to gamble with your heart.

Reuben was eternally thankful, he dared to take the risk.

AUTHOR BIO

Rosie Chapel lives in Perth, Australia with her hubby and three furkids. When not writing, she loves catching up with friends, burying herself in a book (or three), discovering the wonders of Western Australia, or — and the best — a quiet evening at home with her husband, enjoying a glass of wine and a movie.

Website http://rosiechapel.com/
Facebook
https://www.facebook.com/RosieChapelTheAuthor/
Twitter @RosieChapel2015
Goodreads https://www.goodreads.com/rosiechapel_author

For your further enjoyment... I hope... I have included an excerpt from *All At Once It's You* — the book in which Reuben is first introduced.

The list and synopses of my other books follow this snippet.

ALL AT ONCE IT'S YOU

EXCERPT FROM CHAPTER THREE

Alex walked for about an hour, returning to the house feeling invigorated, hoping she would be able to do the same every morning. Ensuring the wicket was latched securely, Alex unclipped the dogs, wiped their feet on a towel, which seemed suited to the purpose, and let them into the warmth of the kitchen. Then she strolled over to her end of the house, leaving her wet shoes on the doormat. Indulging in a quick shower, she was pleased to note the heat from the water, on top of the walk, loosened the last of her tight muscles.

Alex knew she wouldn't be required to dress in a suit, but still dithered over the appropriate attire of a research assistant. Eventually, choosing a pair of dark green chinos, a sage green, long sleeved T, and a hip-length chunky-knit cardigan. It was cool at the moment but if it was anything like yesterday it was unlikely to stay that way. Making her way to the kitchen, Alex pottered about, boiling the kettle, and hunting out what seemed likely prospects for breakfast. Then, she did what she most desired the previous evening — went into the lounge and made a beeline for the books.

When Reuben stuck his head around the door, half an hour or so later, she was far away in the first century AD, a book on Vespasian's rule catching her eye. It took her employer two attempts to attract her attention, waving off her stammered apologies.

"I'm always pleased when those books come off the shelves. While I'm in the middle of a new project, any I'm not using tend to get neglected," he chuckled. Replacing the one she was reading in its allocated spot, Alex joined Reuben in the kitchen where they chatted over breakfast, Alex explaining she'd taken the dogs for a walk, hoping he didn't mind.

"I found their leashes and didn't let them off. It was perfect, just the dogs and me — not another soul to be seen."

"They will go for as many walks as people will take them, and they'll love you forever," Reuben assured, as the oldest one, came to lean on Alex while she was eating. Alex ruffled his fur. "That's Ben, he's just registering his interest aren't you, mate?" Ben merely fixed his huge dark eyes on the woman whom he was certain would fall for his doggy charms.

"Patience, Ben," she grinned. "At least give me chance to eat some of it." Ben's tail swished on the stone flags and he settled on the floor by her feet. The other three — Pip, Coco, and Gus, as introduced by Reuben — formed an orderly and ever hopeful queue behind Ben, determined not to miss out.

Once the kitchen had been set to rights, the dishwasher stacked, each of the four, not-so-patient, dogs given a tasty treat, and after Alex finished getting ready for the day, she made her way along to the office. Reuben was already seated at one of the desks, but stood to explain what he wanted Alex to get started on. When asked, Reuben assured her, he didn't mind if she listened to music through head-phones, as long as the work was done. Flicking her iPod to her favourite mix of tunes, Alex quickly became absorbed in her task, and neither heard a car pull up, the front door slam, or the heavy footfall along the stone passage.

The door swung open.

A tall, dark-haired man came in, his eyes scanning the room. Reuben spotted him and stood, a ready smile warming his face. The visitor stared at the young woman seated at the far side, she seemed familiar somehow, but he couldn't place her. Alex remained unaware of his scrutiny; her hand — unconsciously swaying with the music in her head — twirled a pencil, as she concentrated.

"Jake, you're home early. Did you have a good evening?" Reuben interrupted his son's contemplation.

"Thanks, I did. Who's this now?" Frowning in Alex's general direction.

"This is Alex Mallory. I told you I was hiring an assistant; don't you ever listen?"

"Of course, I listen, but you said … ahhhh, right … I get it."

"What are you blithering about, son?" Reuben looked confused; his mind already drifting back to the documents he'd been reading.

"Yeah, you told me an Alex was coming. I assumed it was a man." Jake's tones were irritated.

"Still hung up on this, Jake? She was the best applicant, what was I supposed to do? Reject her, in the hopes a bloke might eventually apply for the position, all because of what happened last time. I haven't had one single male apply, and I can't keep waiting. I have deadlines. Don't worry about me, Alex isn't like that."

"And how the hell could you possibly know that, Dad?

She must have been here less than twenty-four hours, since you were alone when I left yesterday afternoon." As he said this, the image of a tired young woman, leaning on a car, at the edge of the moor flitted into his mind, and he glanced back at Alex, his brow creasing again.

Almost as though she heard his thoughts, Alex turned her head and Jake was presented with the most ridiculous visage.

In the process of deciphering some text, she was wearing magnifying glasses in order to read the characters more easily. They made her eyes bug out and seem enormous, totally hiding the rest of her face, and despite his annoyance, Jake couldn't help himself. He burst out laughing.

Immersed in history and classical music, something made Alex glance across the room. The magnifying glasses made anything beyond about three inches in front of her all blurry, but she was pretty sure there was an extra person in the room. Then she heard a bark of laughter and, puzzled, removed the glasses, blinking as her eyes adjusted.

She felt her jaw drop. It was him. The grumpy driver from the previous afternoon. What was he doing here? One of Reuben's colleagues perhaps? She wasn't really sure what to do, but felt it polite, at the very least, to close her mouth and introduce herself. Taking the tiny buds out of her ears, Alex pushed back her chair and stood. He was laughing; maybe he wasn't grumpy after all. Smiling, in what she hoped was a confident manner, she walked over to him, holding out her hand.

"Hello, I'm Alexandra Mallory, Reu ... Professor Faulkner's very new assistant."

No longer laughing, he ignored her outstretched hand, his eyes boring into her, his expression becoming grim. Alex was nonplussed, wondering what she'd done to cause such displeasure. Her smile died, her hand fell awkwardly to her side, and heat washed up her cheeks.

"Well... err... pleased to meet you... whoever you are," this last muttered under her breath. Apparently unconcerned, Alex turned on her heel, and went back to her desk, stuck her earbuds in, shoved the glasses back on her nose and focussed on the facsimile in front of her, though careful observation might have spotted a tremor in the hand holding the pencil. She didn't want to lose this job.

"Jake," Reuben ground out in fierce undertones. "What is wrong with you? That was plain rude."

"You don't need an assistant, Dad, I could do what she's doing," flicking his hand towards Alex, "all those hours on digs must surely count for something."

"When? When could you? And since when have you ever wanted to? You're an engineer, not a historian. How could you possibly put in the hours I need, to get this book finished by the due date? I can't hang around all day, hoping you might fit me in for a few paltry hours to go through texts and search databases. I need the information as I'm writing, not two weeks later."

It was the same old argument. Jake wanted to help his father, but his job often took him away for days, sometimes months, on end. He loved history, almost as much as Reuben did, but he knew his limitations, and in all honesty, spending all day every day researching, would drive him batty. The last assistant, however, hadn't worked out so well and Jake, who did not want a repeat, was inclined to be over-protective.

To be fair, this Alex person looked less of a problem, for

a start she appeared to be working, rather than trolling through social media pages, or taking selfies, which was all the last assistant, Tricia, seemed capable of. It was difficult getting anyone to come out here — Rosedale Abbey was miles from anywhere and most young people preferred the, relatively, lively centres of Whitby, Scarborough, or York to a sleepy little village. Tricia, despite having admirable computer skills was one such person; the idea of working for an academic, more interesting on paper than in reality. There was also another reason her employment had to be terminated, but neither Reuben nor Jake was about the dredge that up; Jake's comments were enough.

Jake, unwilling to admit he was out of order, said merely, "I'm going to pack a few things, I have to be in Manchester 'til the end of the week. Meetings," when Reuben raised a quizzical brow, "be careful Dad, that's all I ask."

Reuben smiled. "Don't you worry about me son, Alex will work out just fine, you'll see." He patted Jake on the arm, rather absently, as a new train of thought distracted him, and he moseyed back to his desk, fingers soon flying across the keyboard.

Jake grinned, used to his father's absent-minded ways, and was about to leave when movement caught his eye. Alex stood to lean across the desk, reaching for a book at the opposite side, her slender fingers scrabbling to catch the corner. He was about to step over to help, when she managed to grasp it, and as she pulled it towards her, opening it up, her face lit up in a smile of delight. Fascinated, by what seemed almost a ritual, he watched as she lifted the old volume to her nose and inhaled, stroking the page as she set it down. *Maybe she would work out after all.*

Shaking his head to rid it of the image, Jake walked out, letting the door swing quietly closed behind him.

All At One It's You is available worldwide

OTHER BOOKS BY ROSIE CHAPEL

<u>Historical Fiction</u>

The Hannah's Heirloom Sequence

The Pomegranate Tree - Hannah's Heirloom - Book One

Echoes of Stone and Fire - Hannah's Heirloom - Book Two

Embers of Destiny - Hannah's Heirloom - Book Three

Etched in Starlight - Hannah's Heirloom - Prequel

Hannah's Heirloom Trilogy - Compilation – e book only

Prelude to Fate

<u>Regency Romances</u>

Once Upon An Earl - Linen and Lace - Book One

To Unlock Her Heart - Linen and Lace - Book Two

Love on a Winter's Tide - Linen and Lace - Book Three

A Love Unquenchable - Linen and Lace - Book Four

A Hidden Rose - Linen and Lace - Book Five

The Daffodil Garden

His Fiery Hoyden - A Regency Novella

A Regency Duet

A Regency Christmas Double

Fate is Curious

<u>Contemporary Romances</u>

Of Ruins and Romance

All At Once It's You

Cobweb Dreams

Just One Step

Anthologies

Love Kindled - Building Love

Winning Emma - With Love From London - VOTH: Vol 1

A Love Impossible - With Love from Dublin – VOTH: Vol 3

A Guardian Unexpected – Unconditional

Chasing Bluebells - Wicked Spawns A Legacy of Evil

HISTORICAL FICTION

The Pomegranate Tree
Hannah's Heirloom ~ Book One

Hoping to trace the origins of an ancient ruby clasp, a gift from her long dead grandmother, Hannah Wilson travels to the fortress of Masada with her best friend, Max. Strange dreams concerning a rebel ambush begin to haunt Hannah and following a tragic accident, she slips into the world of Ancient Masada.

A woman out of time, Hannah must rely on her instincts and her knowledge of what will befall this citadel to survive. Will she escape, or is she doomed to die along with hundreds of others as Masada falls – and what does any of this have to do with an ancient ruby clasp?

Echoes of Stone and Fire
Hannah's Heirloom ~ Book Two

Pompeii - a vibrant city lost in time following the AD79 eruption of Vesuvius. Now rediscovered, archaeologists yearn for an opportunity to uncover the town's past. Some things, however, are best left alone - revealing the secrets hidden beneath the stones could prove perilous. Hannah and Max are brought to Pompeii by a surprise invitation to join an excavation team who are trying to uncover the city's long history.

After entering an excavated house that bears a Hebrew inscription, Hannah's two worlds collide, and she falls back through time to ancient Pompeii. A place where her ancestor is a physician to gladiators engaged in mortal combat, where riotous mobs run amok and where a ghost from the past returns to haunt her.

Will Hannah and her loved ones manage to escape the devastation she knows is coming, before the town is engulfed in volcanic ash? Will she ever find her way back to Max the love of her life, waiting not so patiently millennia away? Or will echoes be all that remain?

Embers of Destiny
Hannah's Heirloom ~ Book Three

AD80 ~ Hannah and Maxentius must embark on a new journey to Northern Britannia. This harsh frontier is far from the comforts of Rome and danger lurks where least expected; a garrison of soldiers, some unhappy with their isolated posting; local tribes, outwardly accepting of their Roman occupier, but who may still resent the seizure of their lands.

Millennia away, Hannah Vallier finds a familiar item while working in a museum near Hadrian's Wall. It is the pomegranate; carved by Maxentius on Masada. Before Hannah can discuss it with Max, disaster strikes! Believing her husband has been killed, Hannah retreats into the past, her soul melding with that of her ancestor, but with little idea of what they could face. Is the risk from the conquered tribes, or much closer to home?

As rebellion threatens to shatter a fragile peace, Hannah's heart whispers that just maybe Max isn't dead and that he is calling her home. Can she trust her heart, or will she remain caught out of time, her destiny floating away like embers on a breeze?

Etched in Starlight
Hannah's Heirloom ~ Prequel

Maxentius ~ a Roman soldier fresh from the battlefields of Armenia, arrives to take command of the military outpost of Masada, Herod's isolated citadel in the Judaean desert. A seemingly mundane posting after years of warfare, Maxentius finds it more challenging to maintain a focused garrison than to face the wrath of the Parthians across a disputed frontier.

Hannah ~ a young Hebrew physician spends her days dealing with injuries from street brawls, deprivation, disease and loss. As her beloved Jerusalem plunges into chaos; her brother — who belongs to a band of rebels determined to drive out their Roman occupiers — tells her of their plans to storm a desert fortress and steal the weapons stored there, persuading his reluctant sister to go with him.

Masada ~ following the ambush, Hannah finds and treats three badly wounded Roman soldiers. In the aftermath and against impossible odds, Hannah and Maxentius realise that they are more than healer and captive, their fate already etched in starlight.

Prelude to Fate

For Lucia, staring into the jaws of an horrific death, escape seems impossible.

Rufius Atellus, a veteran Roman soldier, is appalled when he recognises one of the victims about to be executed. Surely this is a ghastly mistake?

A ferocious she-wolf, anticipating a tasty meal, suddenly finds herself under a human's control.

In an unexpected twist, and as danger threatens, the lives of all three become inextricably entwined. Was it chance brought them together in that theatre of bloodshed, or simply a prelude to fate?

REGENCY ROMANCE

Once Upon An Earl
A Regency Romance
Linen and Lace ~ Book One

When Fate saw fit to intervene in the life of Giles Trevallier, the very respectable Earl of Winchester, by dropping a female — soaked to the skin and with no memory of who she is or how she came to be there — literally at his feet, no one could have predicted the outcome.

While uncovering her identity, Giles realises he is falling hopelessly in love with his mystery guest, who unbeknownst to him, is succumbing to similar emotions; but, when the heart is involved, a thoughtless word or gesture can thwart even Fate's best-laid plans.

Faced with misunderstandings, whispers of scandal, secret documents and foreign agents, their chance at a happy ever after seems elusive, but fairy tales often happen when least expected, and love — however inconvenient — usually finds a way to conquer all.

To Unlock Her Heart

A Regency Romance
Linen and Lace - Book Two

Abused by a duke, and shunned by Society, relief seems at hand when Grace Aldeburgh is bequeathed a house in a small village, far from malicious gossips.

Once there, a tentative friendship blooms between Grace and Theo Elliott, the local doctor, who has already resolved to be the man to unlock her heart.

Just when happiness appears to be within her grasp, her erstwhile tormentor once again stalks Grace. After a failed kidnap attempt, the duke's quest culminates in an acrimonious confrontation, and the reason for his venal pursuit becomes agonisingly clear.

Love on a Winter's Tide
A Regency Romance
Linen and Lace ~ Book Three

Lady Helena Trevallier is in no hurry to marry, unwilling to allow a man to dictate her life. She has a secret, one that would probably horrify her social set and one any prospective suitor would demand she curtail. Every day, Helena disappears into a world few acknowledge, helping the poor, downtrodden and abused.

Hugh Drummond avoids most of the Society events he is invited to; events stalked by mamas seeking husbands for their daughters. A state of wedded bliss is something that holds no interest for him. Busy managing his shipping line, he sees no need for a wife, whose only joy is dancing and frivolity. If — and it was a huge if — he ever married, he would want a woman as capable as he, not some giddy society Miss.

Then, Hugh meets Helena and despite their resolve,

fate, it seems, has other ideas. As their attraction deepens however, treachery threatens to tear them apart. Will they uncover the perpetrator in time, or will their love be swept away, lost forever on a winter's tide?

A Love Unquenchable

A Regency Romance

Linen and Lace ~ Book Four

Jessica Drummond, a bright and cheerful young woman, rarely gives romance, let alone love, a thought. Long hours working in her brother's shipping office affords little chance of her ever meeting an eligible bachelor.

Duncan Barrington, veteran of the Napoleonic Wars, believes himself wounded in both body and soul. He has no intention of inflicting his demons on anyone, certainly not a beautiful and, in his opinion, irresponsible city lady.

One cold and snowy morning, the plight of a bedraggled puppy throws Jessica and Duncan together and, as a spark of something indefinable yet wholly unquenchable begins to burn, it is unclear who rescued whom.

A Hidden Rose

A Regency Romance

Linen and Lace ~ Book Five

After witnessing his mother's grief at the loss of his father, Nick Drummond resolved never to cause someone he loved such distress. Even the happiness of his siblings would not sway him – until he met Rose.

Rose Archer was almost content assisting her doctor father in a tiny fishing village in the north of Yorkshire. To experience the world beyond, a tantalising dream – until she met Nick.

Unexpectedly, the impossible becomes possible, and the renounced – desired above all things, but the shipwreck that brought them together, may yet tear them apart. Will Nick learn to trust his heart, or will his love for Rose remain forever hidden?

The Daffodil Garden
A Regency Romance

Horrifically scarred during the war, William Harcourt - Marquis of Blackthorne - prefers to spend his days in the quiet of his daffodil garden; plants do not pity, turn away, or judge.

Lucy Truscott, whose life is far removed from that of the ton, has no idea that by saving the life of a young woman, to whom she bears an uncanny resemblance, her own will be placed in mortal danger.

A chance encounter leads to something more. William begins to trust that Lucy sees the man beneath the scars, while Lucy is persuaded that love might actually transcend status.

Unfortunately, before their courtship has really begun, someone has every intention of ending it - permanently.

His Fiery Hoyden
A Regency Novella

A plea for help ignored. A child left to bring up her baby brother.

Livvy has no respect for the nobility; they let her down

when she most needed them. Why should she accede to their demands now?

Philip, Lord Harrington, is stunned to discover the young heir to the dukedom lives a stone's throw away in a ramshackle cottage, and resolves to restore the child to his birthright.

They meet in a clash of wills, but just when it seems Livvy might surrender, the victory Philip desires, may not taste all that sweet.

A Regency Duet

Luck be a Pirate
(first published in the Kiss My Luck Anthology)

Luck wasn't something retired pirate Kennet Alexson believed in – good or bad. However, even he had to concede that landing a job at Trentams shipyard, and meeting Lynette Collins, was more than coincidence.

Fortune it seemed, was smiling on him for once.

As Kennet adjusts to life on dry land, his friendship with Lynette deepens into something far more enduring, and what once seemed elusive now becomes possible.

Unfortunately, fate has other plans, and Kennet's good luck is about to run out.

The Highwayman's Kiss
(first published in the Once Upon a Love anthology)

Nothing exciting had ever happened to Juliette St Clair. Her days were spent assisting her father or calling on friends, wandering art galleries, taking constitutionals or, and more preferably, escaping into her books. Her evenings her evenings — an endless round of balls, where she preferred to remain invisible.

Until the day she was robbed by a highwayman.

A Regency Christmas Double

Heart Rescued
(originally published in the Tales for the Season Anthology)

Four years since Jasper lost the woman he was hoping to marry. Four years since he closed his heart and withdrew from Society. He has no idea his reclusive existence is about to be shattered.

Enter his sister's best friend, Harriet, a flame haired beauty, who needs his help.

Reluctantly he agrees and as they spend time together, it is clear their feelings run deep.

Although Harriet affects Jasper in a way no woman ever has, he believes her to be out of his league ~ but it's Christmas and she might just be the one to melt his frozen heart

Catch a Snowflake

Romance often blossoms in the most unlikely of places - but in a ward full of wounded soldiers - surely not?

When Lucas Withers comes face to face with Jemima Parsons - a young woman who blames him for her brother's injury - falling in love is the last thing on their minds.

What neither of them anticipated, was the magic of snowflakes.

Fate is Curious

Happily, ever after? No such thing! Bereft, following her beloved husband's sudden death, Lady Charlotte Sherbrooke has lost her belief in such romantic nonsense.

Successful shipping merchant, Zacharie Romain, is no stranger to loss; his business can be hazardous. Moreover, his wife died in childbirth and even though it happened a decade ago, he has no mind to expose himself to such sorrow again.

They meet in less than joyful circumstances but, as the year turns and grief diminishes, the woes of a small boy become the catalyst for something wholly unexpected. Can Charlotte and Zacharie trust what Fate has in store or will past heartbreak prevent them from taking a chance on love?

CONTEMPORARY ROMANCE

Of Ruins and Romance

Kassandra Winters has intrigued Gabriel St Germain since he accidentally knocked her flying outside her university professor's office. Her face haunts his dreams, yet he never expected to see her again. So, he is surprised when she appears, as though destined to do so, in the middle of a ruin, and he concocts a plan to win her heart.

Gabriel's old-fashioned courtship touches something deep inside Kassie and, although struggling to believe someone as handsome as Gabriel could possibly be interested in her, she soon realises she has fallen irrevocably in love with him. However, just as Kassie shares everything of herself with Gabriel, her world comes crashing down.

Can their romance survive, or will it fall in ruins, like the relics of antiquity that brought them together?

All At Once It's You

When Alex arrives in the small village of Rosedale Abbey, to take up a position as a research assistant for a renowned archaeologist, the last thing she is looking for, or expects to find, is love.

Jake was perfectly happy with the status quo. When it came to relationships, he didn't do committed or long term. He called the shots, and if his current flame didn't like it, she knew what to do. A philosophy, which served him well - until he met Alex.

Romance blooms, but even as the untamed wilderness of the North Yorkshire moors weaves its spell, a long-buried secret might yet jeopardise their happily ever after.

Cobweb Dreams

A holiday on the Scottish isle of Mull was just the break Chloe Shepherd needed, an escape from her boring office job and her complete lack of anything resembling a social life. Romance, it seems, isn't on the cards and, although Chloe dreams of finding her soulmate she is beginning to believe love is like cobwebs — spun overnight, only to vanish in the early morning breeze.

Under sufferance, Dominic Winters makes a flying visit to Mull to check on a rental property owned by his family. He hasn't got time for this — so indulging in a holiday fling is the last thing on his mind.

A lamb stuck in a bog proves a most unexpected match-maker and, while Mull weaves its magic, Chloe wonders whether those fragile cobwebs might be far more stubborn than she thought.

Just One Step
(originally published in the Tempting Fate anthology,

In the aftermath of an horrific car accident, Daisy Forrester travels to Italy - hoping, so far from her memories, she might begin to heal.

Archaeologist, and single father, Adam Willoughby is too busy looking after his young daughter to give romance let alone love, a thought.

Neither expects a chance encounter in an ancient ruin to be anything more, but sometimes, that's all it takes.